HEAVENLY

A brilliant shower of stars burst open over the darkening sky. "The first firework! Ah, it is lovely!" She wetted her handkerchief in the water and wrapped it around her sore hand, looking up in wonder.

A second firework, a crimson streak of light, pierced the heavens and exploded into more stars. "Oh! Ah!" Her lips parted and her eyes glowed.

Dear God. Lord William reminded himself that she had tried his patience, tested his resolve, and tempted him beyond all belief. But he could not resist her at that moment.

He leaned forward and kissed her full on the lips.

Emma rocked back on her seat and gasped. "Oh! I liked that better than fireworks!"

He kissed her again. And again.

BOOK YOUR PLACE ON OUR WEBSITE AND MAKE THE READING CONNECTION!

We've created a customized website just for our very special readers, where you can get the inside scoop on everything that's going on with Zebra, Pinnacle and Kensington books.

When you come online, you'll have the exciting opportunity to:

- View covers of upcoming books
- Read sample chapters
- Learn about our future publishing schedule (listed by publication month *and author*)
- Find out when your favorite authors will be visiting a city near you
- Search for and order backlist books from our online catalog
- Check out author bios and background information
- Send e-mail to your favorite authors
- Meet the Kensington staff online
- Join us in weekly chats with authors, readers and other guests
- Get writing guidelines
- AND MUCH MORE!

Visit our website at
http://www.kensingtonbooks.com

A SUMMER'S DAY

LISA NOELI

ZEBRA BOOKS
KENSINGTON PUBLISHING CORP.
www.kensingtonbooks.com

ZEBRA BOOKS are published by

Kensington Publishing Corp.
850 Third Avenue
New York, NY 10022

All Kensington titles, imprints and distributed lines are
available at special quantity discounts for bulk purchases
for sales promotion, premiums, fund-raising, educational,
or institutional use.

Special book excerpts or customized printing can also
be created to fit specific needs. For details, write or phone
the office of the Kensington Special Sales Manager: Attn.
Special Sales Department, Kensington Publishing Corp.,
850 Third Avenue, New York, NY 10022. Phone: 1-800-
221-2647.

Zebra and the Z logo Reg. U.S. Pat. & TM Off.

First Printing: March 2005
10 9 8 7 6 5 4 3 2 1

Printed in the United States of America

For Mrs. Shady

CHAPTER 1

She had taken over his favorite chair. There seemed to be nothing Lord William could do about it. He glared at the Egyptian cat, to no avail.

Nefret responded with a golden-eyed glare of her own before she yawned and settled her nose inside her elegant tail. She was beautiful, with sleek fur the color of desert sand.

At least the chair was covered in canvas that her claws could not penetrate, like all the furniture in the room. A vigorous housecleaning was under way at Cranley Hall. Lord William had barely escaped a thwack from a robust footman, who was beating the rugs hung outside for that purpose and who had apologized profusely. Fred had not seen him approach.

He had only just escaped similar perils at his mother's London house. Here, far away in the drowsy Devon countryside, life moved at a more amiable pace and the servants had not thought to clean the house properly until after Lord William's arrival.

Their well-meaning efforts were somewhat wasted on Cranley Hall, which was falling apart faster than it could be repaired. Lord William was of the opinion that only ivy held certain walls together at the corners. The roof leaked intermittently, never in the same place twice, and there was not a level floor in the place.

Still, it was home—one of several that his family owned and his favorite, for all that it was shabby. His travels had kept him away for the better part of several years and the house had not been well kept up.

But that was about to change, given his efforts and those of the servants. Even the library would get a thorough going-over. Mrs. Diggory, the housekeeper, and Mr. Winkworth, the butler, had nipped in ahead of him and draped everything in canvas.

The maids and the village girls that Mrs. Diggory usually hired to help would follow shortly, wielding mops, brooms, and wet rags like weapons of war.

William smiled ruefully. "They will chase you out into the garden," he said to the indifferent cat. Nefret yawned again. It was an empty threat. He could not let that happen.

His brother Edward, a scholar of antiquities, had asked him to take particular care of her. Edward had added that Nefret was descended from the pets of the pharaohs, animals that the ancients had considered divine.

Preposterous. She meowed like any other cat, cleaned herself each day from nose to tail like any other cat, hunted like any other cat. In fact, Nefret had left him a dead mouse that very morning. On his tea tray. Next to the milk jug, into which she dipped one narrow paw, licking it thoroughly afterwards. Several times.

As a consequence, William had been forced to drink his tea black, which upset his stomach. The cat had gazed at him with those unnerving golden eyes when she tired of tasting the milk, perhaps waiting for him to eat the little delicacy she had so thoughtfully provided.

Ugh. The memory made him shudder.

William had shooed her away and placed a silver dome over the mouse. He had picked at the rest of the breakfast and contented himself with a few bites of toast.

Ominously silent, Nefret had then left the bedroom, waving her tail in a disdainful way. Was it his imagination or was she quieter than other cats? She seemed to come and go like a will o' the wisp, and did exactly as she pleased. No one could catch her, not even Mrs. Diggory, who was partial to cats and fed a few strays on the sly.

William suspected that the housekeeper had treated Nefret to an entire saucer of milk more than once. He would have to talk to her. Better yet, he would have Winkworth do the honors.

After the butler had disappeared with the breakfast tray and Lord William recommenced his perusal of yesterday's papers, William had heard a distant shriek belowstairs, coming from what sounded like the kitchen.

Bertha, the cook, had a fit of temper every time she lost a spoon or some other small thing, and the scream had not troubled him. But Winkworth had informed him later that the cook had nearly fainted upon discovering the mouse, which milord had neglected to mention.

That was because Lord William, deep in a newspaper account of stock transactions which had cost investors most of their money, had forgotten all about the troublesome rodent. He asked Winkworth to convey his apologies to Bertha.

The butler nodded, and then said that Nefret had followed him when he took the dead mouse upstairs to the library, the farthest room from the kitchen. She had watched him every second of the way with fiery golden eyes until he felt a chill up his spine. Nonetheless, he had thrown the disgusting thing into the overgrown garden beneath the windows.

Nefret had obviously remained in the library, hiding under the furniture until the butler left and staying hidden when he returned with the housekeeper to ready the room for cleaning.

No doubt the aristocratic cat assumed that the clean white canvas on her chair—on *his* chair, Lord William thought crossly—had been placed there for her benefit. His niece and nephew loved to spoil her.

William supposed the children regarded the cat as a link to their peripatetic parents, who had also left Caroline and Charlie in his care, going off to visit the pyramids and other things too hot and dry to even think about. But he was very fond of the children and did not mind.

Lord William went to the window, wondering where they were now. The day was fine and a cloudless blue sky arched over the rolling hills of Devon. Cows dotted the green pastures here and there, and an occasional straw hat popped up where a farmer walked his rows, but few people were out in the sun.

He caught a glimpse of a white dress near a hedgerow and heard the distant shouts of children. The dress belonged to Miss Emma Snow, of course—Caro and Charlie's temporary governess—who appeared for only a moment. She walked to the end of the hedgerow and disappeared under the overhanging branches of an old willow by the brook that he knew was there, carrying what seemed to be a picnic basket. Evidently the children would have their lessons and their lunch al fresco. Splendid idea. Sensible girl.

Miss Emma Snow was like no other governess he had ever met. The children adored her. Lord William had understood why within a week of meeting her.

Simply put, Emma was charming, high-spirited, and clever. She was also remarkably pretty. Her manners were refreshingly natural, precisely what one might expect from a well-bred country girl, but a pleasant change indeed from the nervous affectations of London belles.

Her lively mind had obviously benefited from an excellent education in the classical tradition—William's brother had mentioned that much in one of his innumerable letters, as he was most particular about such things. Miss Snow had an intelligent answer for every question the ever-curious children thought to ask.

But Miss Snow had been hired only for the summer in place of the Dreadful Bumpus, Lord William's private name for the old dragon who had been his niece and nephew's governess for the last four years. The Dreadful Bumpus had gone to take the healing waters of Bath for the summer.

Lord William had been delighted to hear of it, and was grateful to be spared the never-ending recital of Mrs. Bumpus's aches and pains—and her fascinating but highly unscientific theories as to their cause.

Did Edward not see that Miss Snow was by far the better choice? Sometimes his brother's nose was too deep in his books for him to see anything that was happening in the present, and his dear wife Elizabeth was not much better.

Charming as Emma was, she had not said much about herself and Lord William wished to know more. Edward had mentioned that she was the only daughter of a vicar, a distant relation of Edward's flighty first wife. That dear lady had died long ago, leaving Edward more than enough money to remarry whom he chose, so long as his new bride was willing to ride on a camel and gallivant all over Egypt.

To no one's surprise, William's brother had chosen Elizabeth Sloan, a plain spinster of admirable intelligence who shared his interest in antiquities. When they were not studying hieroglyphics, they went about the amusing business of procreation like any other married couple. Charlie and Caro had arrived ten and six years ago, to their parents' great joy.

The happy shouts grew louder. That was Charlie, who was no doubt already wading in the brook, trying to catch a bullfrog or filling his straw hat with minnows. Lord William had done much the same at his age on warm summer days.

He had half a mind to join them. Would Miss Snow mind if he did? It would be a delightful way to escape the advancing army of purposeful housemaids and their damned feather dusters, which always made him sneeze.

And it would be a chance to talk to Miss Snow in an informal setting, something he wanted very much to do. . . .

Lord William brought his thoughts back to the present moment, distracted by the appearance of a female figure walking briskly upon the road from town. He could not make out who it was at this distance. He looked about for his spyglass—oh, there it was, on the library table and under an acre of canvas. Bother.

He leaned out the window again and waited for the young woman to draw near enough for him to recognize her.

But the innkeeper's daughter recognized him first. Susie Trelawny spotted him at the window and ran the last quarter-mile, arriving quite out of breath. "Good day, sir!" she panted, looking up. Her hair fell down her back and her light cap went with it.

"Hallo, Susie! What brings you here?"

She dropped the leather bag she held and picked up the cap, all in a swivet. She put it back on her head somewhat askew, patting her tumbling hair back into place as best she could. "Old Blimey's gone! Mind if I look about?"

"Not at all. But why would your cat come here?"

"I don't know. But I met yer stable lad driving the dogcart into town as I was heading out. Robbie said he saw Blimey heading this way." Everyone knew the innkeeper's cat. Blimey had but one eye and one ear, a stump of a tail, and he was as big as a pig.

Susie held up the leather bag. "I brought this to catch him—he won't be able to claw his way out. Me dad will worry himself sick if I don't bring Blimey home."

"I understand." Lord William knew that David Trelawny was proud of his hideous pet, which had bested all the village dogs in one snarling fight after another. The other tomcats did not dare even to look Blimey in the eye.

Susie opened the rusty gate to the overgrown garden, clucking softly as she began to look through the tangled shrubs and vines. "He didn't run away and he has never been scared of anything. Robbie said he was walking slow-like and dignified."

"Perhaps it was one of Blimey's seven sons." The old tomcat had sired many litters bearing his distinctive stripes, though none of his progeny were as big—or as ugly.

"No, sir. Robbie was quite sure. There is only one Blimey."

That was certainly true, and the cat had earned his odd name the hard way. "Blimey!" was what everyone said when they first caught sight of his battered face and impressive girth. People usually stepped aside to let him pass.

Lord William thought with amusement of the way the huge tom swaggered about the inn yard, sniffing at unloaded luggage and even sitting atop it when he felt so inclined. "I am sure he has come to no harm, Susie. Perhaps Mrs. Diggory has been feeding him. But I scarcely think he would travel this far for a saucer of milk."

"Not when *I* give him cream—oh, there he is!" Susie reached into a bush and came up with a handful of leaves. "Blimey! You are very naughty, you are! Come here at once!"

The tomcat sidled into the open and yowled in a deep voice. Behind him, Lord William heard an answering meow, soft and low, from Nefret.

Understanding dawned. His brother and his sister-in-law had stopped at the inn on their way to Cranley Hall three weeks ago. Blimey must have known that there was a female cat in their luggage, and the tomcat had found her at last.

He whirled around to see Nefret perched upon the back of the chair, about to leap out the open window. "Stop!"

Her golden eyes flashed him a look of pure fury. Winkworth had not been exaggerating.

Lord William turned back to the window and closed it quickly, waving good-bye to Susie through the glass. She was preoccupied with wrestling the huge tomcat into the leather bag and did not see him.

Nefret meowed again, for what reason William could not tell. But since he had her attention, he thought it best to keep it. "Allow me to explain, my dear puss. Virtue is a precious thing that, once lost, can never be regained. Therefore, you are confined to the library until I think of a better plan."

The cat jumped down and skulked under another canvas-draped chair until Lord William could see nothing but the tip of her twitching tail. He had no doubt that she was making plans of her own.

Someone knocked on the door and opened it

slowly, evidently not expecting anyone to be inside. William ran to the door and banged it shut.

"I beg your pardon, sir!" said Winkworth anxiously from the hall. "I did not know you were inside—but the maids are on their way. They are in the next room."

Lord William opened the door barely an inch, keeping an eye on the twitching tail. He barred the way with one foot, just in case Nefret intended to escape, and explained the situation to the butler in a few brief words.

Winkworth nodded. "I will ask the girls to clean elsewhere for the time being, milord. We will have to do something about that cat, though."

"Yes, Winkworth. The solution is simple enough. Nefret will have to be confined for a week or two."

"Very good, sir."

"After all, how difficult can it be to keep a cat indoors?"

The butler seemed to be suppressing a laugh. "That depends, sir. What you have here is a lady cat in a very friendly mood and a tomcat what wants to be her friend more than anything. It is a ticklish situation."

"Indeed it is, Winkworth."

The butler considered the matter a moment longer. "The children are devoted to Nefret, sir. If she has kittens, you will have to keep them all until Lord Edward and Lady Elizabeth come back from Egypt."

"I hadn't thought of that. We will have to make sure that no one lets her out."

"Leave it to me, sir. I will take care of it."

"Thank you, Winkworth. It is a beautiful day. I

had thought of taking a walk. Perhaps I will stop by the brook and say hello to Caro and Charlie."

The butler smiled. "They will like that, milord."

Opening the door only a few inches more, Lord William managed to trade places with Winkworth, happy to escape from the library himself. He had important things to do.

Such as . . . sit with Miss Snow and the children . . . and investigate the contents of the picnic basket—his meager breakfast had *not* satisfied him— and amuse his niece and nephew with tales of his youthful mischief . . . and while away a dreamy afternoon in the most delightful company he could imagine . . . really, being an uncle was a solemn responsibility.

On his way up the stairs to dress, he wondered if Caro and Charlie had encountered the huge tomcat. Perhaps this was not Blimey's first trip to Cranley Hall. But they had never mentioned the animal, nor had Miss Snow. However, Lord William had a feeling that Blimey would be back.

Someone else would have to explain why.

Emma walked around the picnic cloth, spreading out each corner with the aid of Caroline. They had both removed their shoes and so had Charlie, who had gone one step further and rolled up his breeches to wade.

The boy stood in water that swirled and flowed around his knees, looking under rocks for little creatures to capture. He made a grab now and then, coming up empty-handed, to Emma's relief.

She raised the lid of a large wicker hamper, too heavy for any of them to lift. Robbie had brought it in the dogcart at Mrs. Diggory's request: she had wanted the children out of the house.

Emma's much smaller basket, which she had carried over her arm, held books for the children, and scrap paper and stubby pencils for their lessons. Not that they were likely to pay much attention on so fine a day, but she had brought along what might be required just in case.

Though the picnic entailed extra work for Bertha, the temperamental cook had outdone herself. The hamper was filled to the brim with carefully packed foodstuffs and a large, corked earthenware jug, cool and damp to the touch.

Caroline scampered over and peered inside. "Is there cake?"

"Help me unpack and set the cloth and we shall see." Emma handed the little girl a rolled dish-cloth filled with forks and spoons, lifting out several chipped but serviceable plates next.

Caro commenced putting these into place, tucking a serviette by the side of each plate with a fork and a spoon. She set the extra plates in the middle to hold the food and stepped back to inspect her handiwork. "It needs flowers, Miss Snow."

Emma waved a hand. "Pick a few. Here is an empty jar to put them in."

Charlie waded out of the brook. "That is my collecting jar, not a vase. Mrs. Diggory said I might have it."

The motherly housekeeper had raised five sons, Emma knew, and understood about boys and bugs. Charlie's interest in all things that crept and crawled made the housemaids avoid his room.

Caroline pouted. "We must have flowers, Charlie. It is not a proper table without them."

Her brother laughed. "That will never be a proper table, Caro. It has no legs, for one thing."

The little girl's lower lip trembled. Caroline was a stickler for social niceties. Emma sighed and rummaged through the basket. "Here is an extra cup—a very pretty one. Look, it has a gold rim and a little shepherdess painted upon it. Just the thing!"

Caroline took it from Emma's hand and turned the cup this way and that, looking at it with concern. "It is a bit cracked but it is pretty. Thank you, Miss Snow."

She ran off to gather flowers, returning in a few minutes with a handful of cowslips and poppies. Charlie took the cup to the stream and filled it with water, presenting it to his sister with a gallant flourish and spilling water on her.

The little girl giggled. "Do it again."

"Please fill the cup, Charles. But no more splashing," Emma warned. She did not think Charlie had done it on purpose but he might have. He liked to tease his sister.

The boy did as he was asked, and set the cup carefully in the middle of the cloth. Caroline filled it with her limp bouquet, and both children helped Emma unpack the food.

There were buns, left over from breakfast but still soft. There was clotted cream in a covered dish, and strawberry jam in another jar. Sliced ham and cold chicken rounded out the meal. Emma uncorked the earthenware jug with a loud pop, spilling a few drops on her hand, which she tasted with her tongue, to the children's delight.

"Lemonade!"

"Hurrah!" The thirsty children clapped. She

poured out a cup for each of them, and helped them to the food.

Charles ate quickly and requested seconds, eager to get back to the brook. Caroline dawdled over her meal, though she seemed to enjoy it. Emma wondered if the child had forgotten about the cake.

She had not. "Did you find the cake, Miss Snow?"

Emma laughed. "Yes. At the very bottom. It is in a box of its own, tied with string."

Charlie fished in a pocket and brought out a penknife, which he gave to his governess.

"Thank you, Charles. You are prepared for every eventuality, as usual. But we shall have the cake later." She put the knife into her basket.

"Uncle William says it is important to be prepared. He expects I will have adventures like my father and mother, and become an explorer. But I think I would rather collect bugs."

Caroline shuddered daintily. "What is a splorer, Miss Snow?" she asked.

"Someone who travels all over the world and sees things people have never seen before. They write everything down in books between explorations so that we may read of their adventures and learn."

Caroline nodded absent-mindedly and watched Charlie help himself to a spoonful of jam, which he dropped into the bottom of the jar that Mrs. Diggory had given him. "Ants love jam. Watch this, Caro."

Emma gave him a severe look. "Please put the jar away from the food, Charles." She pointed to a spot that seemed safely distant. "And you may not bring the ants home."

He got to his feet and went over to where she had pointed, setting the jar on its side in the soft earth. Caroline and Emma stacked the plates and cups to one side, first brushing the crumbs in the general direction of Charles's jar. Emma could almost hear the *tromp, tromp, tromp* of tiny ant feet heading that way.

"May I have that old cup to collect water things, Miss Snow?" He pointed to the biggest one, which she gave to him.

Charlie returned to the brook, setting the cup aside and rolling up his breeches again. He entered the water and was soon absorbed by whatever he saw in it. Caroline watched him for a minute, then yawned and rubbed her eyes.

Not surprising. The afternoon had grown warmer and the fragrance of hidden flowers—early roses blooming in the hedgerows, perhaps—was almost intoxicating.

"Read to me, Miss Snow."

"What would you like to hear?"

"The fables. Pick one you like."

Emma reached into the basket, bringing out a collection of Aesop with engraved pictures that Caroline enjoyed. The little girl could read well enough, but she loved to hear stories all the same, unlike Charlie, who was too restless to sit still for long.

Nonetheless, Emma had brought Bewick's *Quadrupeds* for him, which she had found in Lord William's library, thinking it suitable for a young naturalist.

His lordship's library was most impressive, though the cluttered shelves sagged and the books were not in order. The *Quadrupeds* had been leaning against a leather-bound set of Shakespeare, in fact. She had thought he would not mind if she borrowed a few books for the children.

The servants could set the books to rights as they cleaned—no, of course not. With the exception of Mrs. Diggory and Winkworth, most of them could not read. Perhaps she might volunteer for this task. It would be an excellent way for Caroline to practice alphabetical organizing; and Charlie could practice patience, a virtue in which he was somewhat lacking.

Yet he was an intelligent, good-hearted boy and his enthusiasm for learning more than made up for it. Without siblings of her own, Emma found that she enjoyed the Kent children very much. They had been well if strictly brought up, and Mrs. Diggory, who was an old dear, was happy to look after them for an hour or two now and then.

Emma leafed through the fables, noticing that Caroline's eyes were drifting shut. The story would have to wait while the little girl napped. Emma wanted to digest—and to think. She set the book to one side.

She looked about her, enjoying the verdant beauty of the site and the fresh air. Though she could not see him, the sounds of splashing and tuneless whistling reassured her that Charles was nearby and happily occupied.

Emma was glad that her father had agreed to let her work as a governess. Her position was humble, but the Kents, who valued education above all, treated her well. However, she had scarcely had time to get to know Lord Edward or his wife before coming to Cranley Hall with the children and meeting their unmarried uncle.

With his dashing good looks, Lord William might have stepped from the pages of a romance novel. He was nothing like his brother.

He had been most kind, inquiring each night at dinner as to her day and the children. The questions did not vary much and were never too personal. Had the children behaved? And what were they learning? Caroline and Charles seemed very fond of their uncle and he obviously adored them.

She wondered whether Lord William had plans to marry and set up a nursery of his own, but of course this was not the sort of question governesses asked. Her mother, however, would have had the answer from him—or someone else—in no time.

Mrs. Snow was extraordinarily good at extracting such information. She hoped that Emma might marry well and did her utmost to investigate all possibilities. Emma's father had not wanted his only daughter to leave the cozy vicarage where his little family abided in harmony, but his wife had persuaded him to let the girl go. It was only for a summer, after all—and that was the only reason Papa had agreed.

Did Mama consider Lord William a catch? She knew he was not likely to inherit the title or the Kent estates, though he seemed to be the master of Cranley Hall.

Lord Edward, Emma's employer, lived many miles away in a grand house of his own. He was older than William by several years and had been left wealthy by his first wife. And there was another, still older, brother who lived exclusively in London and never came to Devon at all, Emma knew.

Their father, the earl, lived in dissolute splendor with his French mistress and sent all his sons money from Paris when he had any. The countess, a pious woman who refused to divorce her philandering husband, lived quietly in Mayfair with her unmarried sister.

The tireless Mrs. Snow had found all this out within days, from a mysterious source she refused to identify. Even given her penchant for exaggeration, much of it was undoubtedly true.

But Emma's father had sniffed upon hearing it. He dismissed the information as idle gossip and chided his wife for repeating it in front of their daughter.

It all seemed quite unreal to Emma, as if the London branch of the Kent family were but characters in a novel—the sort of novel her parents did not want her to read.

Certainly William and Edward seemed to lead blameless lives. But, according to Mrs. Diggory, William did travel to London to see to his investments and visit his mother from time to time.

Had she inherited her mother's gift for finding things out? Emma smiled ever so slightly and stroked Caroline's hair. The little girl had fallen asleep and slumped against her.

Emma moved the child gently onto the cloth, hoping that Caroline would not wake up cranky, as she often did.

A few clouds had drifted into the sky. Emma rolled over into the grass—it was warm and dry and she need not fear staining her white dress— and stretched out to watch them.

She heard the sound of Charles returning, splash by splash. He reached the bank of the brook near where she lay, and scrambled up it with his collecting cup.

"Look what I have found!"

Oh, dear. Emma hoped it did not have too many legs.

He stuck the cup under her nose. She could just see a tiny creature at its bottom, some sort of aquatic insect. The cup also held a few minnows, swimming energetically round and round.

"It is a caddis fly, Miss Snow. See—it builds its own house from bits of rock and sand. Each one is different."

"That is most interesting, Charles. Do you want to draw it? I was thinking that you could begin a record of your investigations into natural history."

Charlie beamed. "Yes, Miss Snow. I could ask Uncle William for a notebook. He is always writing in one himself."

"Very good, Charles." The boy's restlessness in the schoolroom might well improve out-of-doors, she thought, especially if he could study things that interested him. "There are pencils and paper in my basket."

He set down the cup and looked inside the basket, taking out the drawing things and the *Quadrupeds*. "Oh! This is Uncle's book—but he would not let me take it from his library. He must like you, Miss Snow."

Ah . . . what could she say to that? Emma had not asked Lord William's permission but simply assumed that he would not mind. Best to ignore the remark, as Charles meant nothing by it. "Then you must be very careful not to dirty the pages or tear them."

"I will be." He sat cross-legged, the caddis fly and minnows in the cup forgotten for the moment, and leafed through the book, pausing to admire the handsome black-and-white engravings on each page. "Perhaps I will collect animals and not bugs. I could be an explorer at the same time."

"You will have an interesting life no matter which you choose, Charles," Emma said. She brushed a wayward strand of hair from Caroline's face and the child stirred slightly in her sleep.

Emma wondered whether they should be thinking about returning home. On such a peaceful day, time seemed to stand still, one moment flowing into the next as they basked in the warm sun.

Since Charles was absorbed in his book, she might read a few pages of her own. But Emma decided against it and simply shut her eyes.

The sun was only slightly lower in the sky when she opened them. She had not dozed off for long. She looked around for Charles, who had set the *Quadrupeds* aside and was looking into his cup.

Bothered by a gnat, Caroline woke with a start. "Oh—where am I?"

Emma smoothed her hair. "With us, darling. By the brook."

Caroline sat up, sleepy-eyed, her dress crumpled. "Where is Charlie?"

"Over here," her brother replied. "Look, I have caught a caddis fly. Come and see."

The little girl scrambled over on all fours and peered into the cup. "That little thing at the bottom?"

"Yes—let me show you." He reached in with two fingers and pulled it out.

Caroline squeaked with disgust. "Ugh! It is horrid! And wet!"

"A few drops of water won't hurt you, Caroline," Emma said reprovingly. "In any case, if you don't like it, you don't have to look at it. Come here."

Caroline got to her feet and did as she was told, sitting primly by her governess. Charlie gave his sister a sly look. "I have caught a millipede too. It is big and wiggly and horrider, Caro."

So that was how he had occupied himself while she dozed. Emma wished now that she hadn't.

Caroline shrank against her side. "No! I hate sillypedes!"

"*Milli*pedes, you mean." The boy reached into a small pile of leaves at his side and picked up the nasty thing between finger and thumb, brandishing it at his sister.

"Save me, Miss Snow!" Caroline flung herself into Emma's lap and hid her face.

"Now, now." She patted the frightened little girl on the back. "Charlie, put the millipede back under the rock it came from."

"Must I?"

"Yes."

He got up and went to the place where the jar still lay, releasing the millipede into the woods, to Emma's great relief. She noticed that Caroline was peeping at her brother from the folds of Emma's dress, more curious than scared by now.

"You mustn't be afraid of such little creatures, Caroline. A millipede is not very pretty but it will not harm you."

Caroline sat up and threw her brother a look of righteous indignation. "He might."

"Now, Caro—" Emma broke off when the little girl suddenly got to her feet and chased her brother toward the brook. Charlie only laughed, dodging his sister's attempt to slap him—but he slipped on the muddy bank and fell headlong into the water.

"Oh!" Caroline's eyes went wide. "I am sorry, Charlie! I did not mean—"

Spluttering, furious, Charlie stood up and went for his sister, pulling her into the brook and pushing her down. Caroline sat in water up to her waist and howled.

"Children! Shame on you both!" Emma scurried over and hit the same muddy patch that had unbalanced Charles. She too slipped into the water but got a good grip on Caroline as she righted herself.

They were all drenched, shouting and laughing. And that was how Lord William found them.

CHAPTER 2

"Well, well. You seem to be amusing yourselves," Lord William said. He towered above them on the bank, hands on his hips. He grinned——but at least he was not laughing. Not yet.

Emma felt dreadfully embarrassed. Her white muslin dress was clinging to her legs in a most unseemly way and she had no doubt that her face and hands were muddy.

Caroline let out an even more dramatic howl.

"Oh, do stop that," Emma said crossly. "You are not injured, only wet. If you had not chased your brother, he would not have fallen, and we would not all be sitting in this brook."

"Ah. I thought perhaps you were teaching the children to swim, Miss Snow."

Emma shook her head. "With their clothes on? No, my lord. I do not know how to swim in any case."

"I do," said Charlie cheerfully. "Uncle William taught me."

Lord William reached out a hand to Emma. "Allow me, Miss Snow."

She had not let go of Caroline and the two of them got up together. The little girl seemed happy to see her uncle and wound herself around his leg when they reached the dry grass.

"I am soaking wet!" she announced.

"So you are. But the day is warm and there is a breeze. You will soon be dry." He picked up his niece and swung her to and fro. "Does that help?"

The little girl giggled with glee. "Do it again!"

Emma stood to one side and wrung out her dress as discreetly as she was able. Lord William was not looking at her, but playing with Caroline. No. Caroline had flopped down into the warm grass, still giggling, and he *was* looking at Emma. She straightened up.

Do not gawk at her, Lord William told himself. *You have seen many women just as God made them. But never one so lovely,* he added silently.

Emma's brief immersion in cold water had brought a delicate pink into her cheeks and a sparkle to her eyes. Her honey-colored hair was in charming disarray.

He could not help but smile at her. Despite her efforts, the gauzy dress still clung to her thighs— what beautifully rounded thighs!—all the way down to her slender ankles. She was barefoot, he noticed. Miss Snow blushed deeply under his gaze and looked away.

"Well—here we have two wet children and a bedraggled governess. I am not sure what to do next. Miss Snow, what do you think?"

Emma picked up her shoes and stockings but decided against putting them on, propriety aside.

Her dress and drawers were simply too wet. There was no sense in ruining every article of clothing she owned. "I suppose we must return," she said.

"Mrs. Diggory will tuck you all in bed with mustard plasters and bitter tea to ward off colds."

"Oh, dear. Well, then we might as well stay and dry out in the sun, if you are agreeable to that plan."

"Please let us stay!" Charles ran over and tackled Lord William from the side, unable to budge his uncle an inch.

"What's this?" William asked, laughing. "I did not push you in the brook, Charlie. But I am glad to hear that you were not the cause of this mishap—or there would be consequences, my boy."

"It was Caro's fault," Charlie said peevishly.

"Now, now. Do not tattle. I expect you to behave like a gentleman. And you have done something wrong." He pointed to Bewick's *Quadrupeds*, left open on a rock. "You were not permitted to take that book, and yet you did."

Charlie looked from his uncle to his governess without saying a word.

"I took it, my lord," Emma spoke up. "I thought it would interest Charles and I did not know that he was not allowed to remove it from your library."

"I see," Lord William said gravely. But there was a twinkle in his eye. "But I would have let you take it, Miss Snow, had you asked."

"My apologies. You were—not anywhere about, and the children were eager to set out on our picnic."

"I understand."

"It is a very good book, uncle. I think I want to collect animals instead of bugs now."

Lord William shook his head. "Dear me. Cranley Hall might boast its own menagerie someday."

"Yes," Charlie said eagerly. "Could we have a giraffe?"

"I understand that they have a habit of looking into second-story windows, Charlie. Your little sister might not like that."

Still flat on her back, Caroline spoke from the grass. "I would, though. I have always wanted a giraffe. There are animals in the clouds, Uncle William. Come and look."

He bowed ever so slightly to Emma. "Pray excuse me, Miss Snow. The clouds need watching."

Lord William went over to his niece and sat down, his hands clasped over his knees. "What do you see, Caro?"

She pointed up. "A hippogriff—there."

Charlie snorted. "There are no hippogriffs, silly."

"There are in the sky. Clouds can be anything, Charlie," Emma said quietly.

"I see a cloud horse," Lord William said. "It's galloping toward us." A breeze had sprung up, lending truth to his fancy. A fluffy white shape with a streaming tail was moving overhead.

"I see a cloud millipede," Charlie said. His sister ignored his teasing and snuggled against her uncle's side.

"Charles, that will do," Emma said firmly. "Come and help me look through the hamper. Perhaps your uncle would like something to eat. There is quite a bit of food left and we never opened the cake box."

Lord William reclined at his ease. "I would very much like something to eat. My breakfast was spoiled, thanks to that dratted cat. She left a dead mouse upon the tea tray."

Caroline giggled. "Did you eat it, Uncle?"

"I did not. Nefret seemed most put out. She is not speaking to me at the moment."

"Papa told us that she is a royal cat," Caro said.

"So I understand," Lord William said dryly. "But she has friends in low places. The innkeeper's cat paid a call upon her this morning."

"Do you mean old Blimey?" Charlie asked. "He is the biggest cat I have ever seen."

"And where did you see him, Charles? Surely you have not wandered as far as the inn," Emma said. She put some ham and the remains of the chicken on a plate and added a bun. Charles passed it to his uncle.

"He came to the house yesterday, too."

"Did you witness his appearance, Miss Snow?"

"No. But Charles did mention it."

Lord William had a sinking feeling. Perhaps Blimey had already answered Nefret's siren call. Well, there was nothing for it. He, Lord William, had done what he could to protect her virtue.

"I recognized him," Charlie continued. "When we stopped at the inn before coming on to Cranley Hall, he sniffed our luggage and sat on top of Nefret's basket. She meowed at him. I wonder what she was saying."

"That was a few weeks ago," Lord William said, with a mouthful of ham. "How the devil did he find his way here after so long?"

"Perhaps he is in love with Nefret," Caroline said dreamily. "How romantic!"

"Whatever do you give her to read, Miss Snow? Not novels, I hope."

"Of course not. Caroline reads what every little girl reads: her grammar and Bible stories and the fables of Aesop and fairy tales. Oh, I suppose it was *Puss in Boots* that gave her such an odd notion. But that is not a love story, is it?" Emma laughed as she uncorked the lemonade jug and poured a cup for Lord William.

"Thank you, Miss Snow. I believe it is not. Caro is an imaginative child."

"What does that mean?" Caro asked. "Is there cake?"

"Yes," Emma said. She had cut the string around its box and was slicing it with Charles's penknife. Caroline got to her feet and came over.

Making sure the slices were the same size, Emma put each on a plate and let the children find their own forks. There was no sound for a minute or two but contented eating and the clink of silver on china. She cut two more slices, one for herself and one for Lord William.

He took his with a courteous nod, just as if they were sitting at the great table in the dining room of Cranley Hall, not half-on and half-off the picnic cloth.

"Ah, pound cake. My favorite. Is there jam to go with it?"

"Charlie gave it to the ants."

"Well, not all of it, Caroline. I think there is more. Let me see." Emma reached into the hamper and brought out the jam jar, which she uncapped. She dipped a spoon into it and took a deliciously big dollop, holding the spoon in midair for a fraction of a second.

She looked as if she were about to pop the dripping jam into her pretty mouth. Instead, she reached over and spooned it onto his cake.

"Thank you, Miss Snow." His tone was slightly gruff. *If the children were not here,* he thought, *I would like to see you eat that jam—and kiss the sweetness on your lips.*

But the children were there. And such thoughts were hardly proper. Lord William gobbled the rest of his cake, choking a little on the crumbs.

"Would you like some lemonade?" she asked.

"Yes, th-thank you."

She poured him the last of it, watching the last drop fall from the lip of the jug with a little smile. "More cake?"

Oh, God. Venus herself could not have poured lemonade so charmingly. He coughed. "What? Oh—the cake. Yes, I will have more. But no jam this time. It is excellent jam, of course, but I think I prefer the cake plain."

"As you wish." Miss Snow smiled demurely, and also gave Charles a second piece, knowing it would disappear as quickly as the first. Caroline had only eaten half of hers.

"May I give the rest to the sparrows, Miss Snow?"

"Yes, Caroline."

The little girl walked the little distance to the hedgerow and crumbled the cake into tiny bits.

As soon as she had returned, the sparrows flew down, twittering and fighting over the treat. "You must share!" the little girl called.

"Caro, the birds don't know that," Charlie said. "Besides, I would have eaten it."

Caroline stuck out her tongue at her brother.

"Really, Caro," Lord William said. "You cannot

give birds lessons in manners if you do not remember your own."

Emma laughed. "That is a good lesson, worthy of Aesop himself."

"You promised me a story, Miss Snow." Caroline tugged at her sleeve.

"So I did. I shall read to you before bedtime. But we should be going home. Robbie said he would come back for the hamper when the shadows grew long."

Charlie groaned and looked longingly at the remainder of the cake.

"No more. Help pack up the things and do rinse the ants out of that jar. Mrs. Diggory will want it back."

He went for the jar and took it to the stream, swishing it in the running water until it was clean.

Caroline brought her plate to Emma, and frolicked about, letting her uncle help Miss Snow. The little girl much preferred setting a pretty table to clearing away dirty dishes.

While Emma put away what was left of the food, Lord William stacked the plates somewhat haphazardly and gathered up the silver with one hand. "Here you are. Thank you very much for sharing your repast. It is a pleasure to see the children so happy." He lowered his voice. "Mrs. Bumpus disapproves of picnics, I believe."

Charlie came back with the clean jar, which he put into the hamper. "Mrs. Bumpus disapproves of everything."

"You were not supposed to hear that, Charlie," Lord William said.

"But I did. And I disapprove of Mrs. Bumpus.

She is always groaning about her rheumatism and things. Why can't Miss Snow stay?"

"We want her to stay forever, Uncle," Caroline chimed in.

Emma's mouth opened with surprise. She had known that the children liked her but not that they liked her that much.

"She knows much more than Mrs. Bumpus and she is very kind," Charles began.

"And Miss Snow is very pretty," Caroline added, as if that clinched it. "And she never wears black."

Lord William laughed. "That decision rests with your parents. But I will tell them what you said in private, if you both promise not to tell Mrs. Bumpus and hurt her feelings." He gave Emma a warm smile. "You have made a great impression in a very short time, I see."

She only shrugged, embarrassed and pleased by the children's praise.

"Caro, would you like to ride home?" Lord William asked.

"Yes, yes!" She clapped her hands.

Lord William swung the eager girl aloft and settled her on his broad shoulders, her little bare feet dangling against his plain linen shirt. He steadied her with one hand and gave the other to Charles, who had come to stand beside him, smiling up at his uncle and his sister.

The affection they had for each other was touchingly clear—and the golden light of afternoon made them look like figures in a painting she had once seen, a rustic allegory of family love. Emma's heart skipped a beat. Was there ever a man more suited for fatherhood? She wondered why he had not yet married and tried to put the thought out of her mind.

Whatever the reason, it was none of her business—and she ought not to think of such things. She would remain at Cranley Hall only for the summer and she would return to her parents' home at its end.

Emma slipped on her shoes, and put her stockings and Caroline's shoes and stockings into her basket, along with the books and the pencils and paper. She handed Charles his shoes, and off they went.

They returned home, first by way of the lane and then by a cowpath, a shortcut recommended by Charles. When Lord William realized that they were going in circles, they decided upon the long way instead and came up the gravel drive together.

Winkworth was waiting.

"Good evening, sir. Good evening, Miss Snow. Master Charles. Miss Caroline."

The butler favored the children with smiles and seemed to take no notice of Emma's still-damp dress and somewhat disheveled appearance. So she did what her mother always recommended in difficult situations: held her head high and pretended everything was just as usual.

"Look! There is another lion!" Caroline, still riding on Lord William's shoulders, pointed to the stone statues that guarded the front stairs.

There had always been two—one had a chipped nose—but tonight there were three. Even in the fading light, Emma could see that the third was somewhat smaller than the stone lions and striped. It looked something like a cat, but it was too big.

"Blimey!" Charles cried.

"Oh, no," Lord William groaned. He slid Caroline from his shoulders and set her upon the ground. "Winkworth, did Nefret escape?"

"No, sir. I put her under a basket when the maids cleaned the library. And afterwards, I locked her inside."

"Susie must not have been able to keep Blimey in the bag," Lord William said. "Unless he walked all the way from the village again. I must say, I admire his determination. Faint heart ne'er won fair kittycat."

"I told you Blimey was in love," Caroline said.

"Should I put that one under a basket as well?" asked Winkworth doubtfully. "I fear he is more than a match for me."

"No. It is growing dark and he is too wily. We must ensure that Nefret stays inside the library."

"She will need to answer the call of nature, sir."

William scowled. "How did that blasted cat come to rule this house? Make her a box of sand for a necessary, if you must."

"You are very kind, Uncle William," Caroline said.

"Humph. I cannot believe that I must invent a privy for a cat."

"But she is royal!"

"Oh, Caro—I know how much you love her. Come, let us go visit the library and see if Queen Nefret has clawed the furniture out of boredom. I expect she needs to be entertained and you know how."

He picked up the little girl again and walked briskly up the stairs, leaving Charlie and Emma to follow. Winkworth brought up the rear. He did not see Blimey padding behind him, nor did he see the huge tomcat slip inside the door only a second before it closed.

A few hours later, the children were in bed. Caro had not forgotten that Miss Snow owed her a story, and Emma read several fables until her own eyes were drifting shut.

Lord William sat in his library, working by candlelight. Winkworth had had one of the footmen, a carpenter's son, cobble together a box and fill it with sand for Nefret's necessary.

She had used it. It reeked. He could not move her and the box to one of the bedrooms for that reason, nor would Bertha let the cat stay anywhere near the kitchen, after the mouse incident. The great rooms were too difficult to secure.

The outbuildings were a possibility but with the grooms and menservants always coming and going from them, Nefret and Blimey would succeed in meeting in no time.

The cat ceased to prowl among the legs of the library chairs and jumped up onto his favorite once again. She meowed softly, ever so softly, giving Lord William a melting look from her golden eyes.

"You know that Blimey is outside, don't you?"

She was silent.

"And there he will remain. I suggest that you go to sleep and not think about him. Blimey lacks a pedigree and he is as poor as a church mouse."

But I love him, her golden eyes seemed to say.

"Nonsense." He waved her away. "I refuse to discuss this. Winkworth will think I have gone mad." He heard the butler's measured tread coming down the hall, bringing his brandy.

Winkworth tapped upon the door and opened it just a crack, looking round to see where Nefret was.

"Be quick about it, man," Lord William said.

The butler eased through the narrow opening and shut the door firmly behind him. "Your brandy, sir."

"Thank you. I need it. The accounts are at sixes and sevens. We have even less money than I thought and I have already asked the servants to work for half wages until things are better."

"Yes, sir," said Winkworth, who had agreed to this plan out of loyalty to Lord William, whom he liked. But the butler would not have done so for the earl, Lord William's father, whom he detested. Winkworth hoped the old man would never return to Cranley Hall.

"There seems to be no end to the repairs that must be made. The doorknobs are falling off and the roof is leaking. We shall have to economize. Alert Mrs. Diggory."

"I will do so in the morning. She has retired for the evening. Good night, sir." The butler bowed and withdrew as cautiously as he had entered.

Lord William raked both hands through his hair, which was already standing up strangely. How had the family finances come to such a pass? And how had he, the third son, come to be entrusted with the responsibility of restoring Cranley Hall to its former grandeur . . . without the wherewithal to do so?

He had a bad habit of taking on the work that no one else wanted to do. Accordingly, his family seemed to assume he could do everything.

It was one thing to live in a big house and quite another to keep it up. His papa sent money through his London solicitors, some of which Lord William lived on and some of which he invested. However, the greater part of the Kent fortune seemed to have already disappeared down the bejeweled décolletage of his father's French mistress. There was not a damned thing William could do about it.

Edward had inherited his first wife's fortune but William would have to marry an heiress—the daughter of a rich brewer, most likely. He had been introduced to two during his last trip to London. They both resembled pug dogs and they both snuffled. He had been exceedingly polite and escaped at the earliest possible opportunity.

Despite his financial difficulties, he yearned for feminine companionship, wanted a wife, hoped for children of his own. But he had yet to meet a woman who did not seem to care first and foremost about money and he had very little to spare.

The usual alternative—a mistress—might prove more expensive than a wife. Anyway, a mistress was to love what an artificial flower was to a blooming rose—not the same, not even remotely.

Certainly no woman of fashion would leave London, a city he hated. What passed for sophisticated society bored him to distraction. He had no interest in gambling, or the theatre, or drinking to excess in the company of stupid young bucks, dressed to kill and sure to vomit upon their fine clothes before the night was done.

His sojourns abroad and in London had taught

him how happy he was in this house, nestled in the green hills of Devon, with the people he knew and had always known.

But Miss Snow was an interesting new development. She was a blooming rose indeed. He could easily fall in love with her. Her intelligence and beauty would grace his house—if Cranley Hall could be prevented from falling down—and she would obviously make an excellent mother.

He considered the matter of children. Caro and Charlie were great fun, but they would go back to their parents, as they always did.

His churchgoing mother would approve of Miss Snow, he knew. She deplored worldly women, but there seemed to be no other sort in London.

However, Emma Snow was penniless or so he gathered, and as he had no fortune himself, he could not very well contemplate a future with her. Love in a cottage was all very well for cottagers, but he could not quite see himself living humbly, with or without her.

He pushed his chair away from his desk and got up to pace the rug. Nefret watched him in silence.

Lord William picked up his glass of brandy and took a sip. "Here's to love, old girl. Not that it ever did anyone any good." He tossed the rest of the brandy down his throat and headed off to bed.

When the clock struck the midnight hour, Blimey was afoot in the shadows of the hall, his measured tread somewhat slower than that of Winkworth. But no one heard the big cat. He went to the library door and sniffed. Very faintly, Nefret meowed.

Blimey stuck a mighty paw under the door and

wiggled it. It did not move. He wiggled it again. The doorknob's old mechanism almost gave way. Blimey had figured out doors long ago, and he went in and out of one that led to the tavern cellar whenever he wanted. He kept his paw where it was and wiggled the library door again.

It swung open. Nefret was waiting.

CHAPTER 3

The day dawned cloudy, and rain seemed imminent. Caroline and Charles were breakfasting with Mrs. Diggory, according to the maid who brought Emma her breakfast on a tray.

She had overslept. The dark morning had been too quiet and the strong winds of the oncoming storm had chased the birds away. The motherly housekeeper understood how restless the children were likely to be, kept indoors all day long, and perhaps this was her way of giving Emma a few moments of peace.

In any case, Emma was grateful. She sipped her tea and munched her toast, saving her egg for last. This had arrived wearing a knitted cozy shaped like a very small, very plump chicken. Mrs. Diggory had made it. Caroline and Charlie each had one, in different colors.

Emma felt honored. Her own egg—and her own chicken-cozy to keep it warm. Small pleasures were indeed best.

She walked about the room once she had finished her breakfast, stretching and swinging her arms. In a few minutes, she would begin her toilette, pick a dress for the day, and put up her hair. For now, her thoughts were her own.

Emma could not forget the picture in her mind of Lord William and the children. She had even dreamed of them . . . a happy dream suffused with serene summer light that vanished all too quickly.

When she married—if she married—Lord William was the sort of man she would want. Not that she was likely to find such a one. The timid curates who trembled before her father seemed to be all that was available. The thought was depressing and made her feel faintly cross.

She told herself to cheer up. One never knew what life might bring and there might be something new around the most familiar corners. Emma went to the clothes-press and considered her choices.

The gray dress matched the weather. But the yellow one would brighten her mood. She took it from the clothes-press and shook out the wrinkles, then donned clean drawers and a light petticoat. However threatening the sky, the air was still very warm.

She managed the dress easily on her own, as it had no back buttons, and dressed her hair quickly, adding a ribbon in matching yellow just for dash.

A knock on her bedroom door made her turn around.

"Come in."

Molly, the kitchen maid, burst in. "Lord William says you are to come at once, miss. There are peacocks in the hall—two peacocks, I think—screaming their heads off." She paused for breath. "And

Lady Barbara has arrived. I am to be her lady's maid."

"Tell him I am coming," Emma said calmly.

The maid withdrew, leaving the door open.

Emma smiled at herself in the mirror. Right again. One never did know what life might bring. She certainly hadn't expected peacocks. And who was Lady Barbara?

Emma stepped carefully around a mountain of luggage and headed for the marble-tiled foyer. There stood a most unusual personage, clad in the voluminous, fussy fashion of the last century, her white hair piled high. She was talking to Lord William.

He caught sight of Emma over Lady Barbara's shoulder—the personage had to be Lady Barbara— and winked.

"Dear little Willy! Are you winking at me?" Lady Barbara patted his cheek.

"Certainly not." He forced a smile.

Emma came into the room.

"My dear Lady Barbara, allow me to introduce Miss Emma Snow, Caroline and Charlie's governess. Miss Snow, this is Lady Barbara, a lifelong friend of the family."

Emma dropped a curtsey. "How do you do, Lady Barbara?"

The unexpected guest swirled and rustled in her silks as she replied with a theatrical wave. "How do *you* do, my dear? William has been telling me all about you. And so have Caroline and Charlie." She clapped her hands. "Come, children."

Emma looked about and spotted them in back

of a gigantic, open-weave wicker basket that was taller than they were.

"Come see the peacocks, Miss Snow," Charles called. "Lady Barbara brought them from a friend's house."

"Yes. The dear duke is a generous man. He said I might take a pair to my next host, if I would but leave."

Lord William stifled a cough at that statement. Emma came forward, stopped by an unearthly cry from inside the basket.

"Ah! Their song! Is not exquisite, Miss Snow?" Lady Barbara asked. She did not seem to expect anyone to say yes.

"I did not know that peacocks made any sound at all," Emma admitted.

"Oh, but they do. They cry and shriek and fly into a fury on very little provocation. They are Barbara's gift to me," Lord William said, rolling his eyes heavenward when that lady was looking the other way.

"Look at the colors of their feathers. They are very beautiful," Caroline said in an awed whisper.

"The peacock is beautiful," Charles said. "The peahen is drab."

"It ought to be the other way around," said Caroline.

"Dear children," Lord William interrupted. "Where shall we put them? Charlie, you wanted a menagerie—these will be our star attraction."

"They can wander about the grounds, you know," Lady Barbara said. "The finest houses boast flocks of peacocks. They are prized for their decorative quality."

"I see," said Lord William. "Perhaps no one will

notice that Cranley Hall is falling down around our ears if we have enough peacocks to distract them. We might need more than two, though. Will these lay eggs?"

Barbara gave him a sad look and a concerned frown. "Is it as bad as all that, Willy? Your mother hinted but I had no idea—"

"I will explain later, if I may." He took Lady Barbara to the foot of the stairs, where Molly waited, decked out in a lace-trimmed cap and apron. Emma marveled at her instantaneous transformation into a lady's maid.

"Of course, Willy." Lady Barbara rustled onto the first step.

"No doubt you wish to rest from your journey. Please join us for lunch at twelve. Caro and Charlie, come give Lady Barbara a kiss."

Caroline complied eagerly, embracing the old lady and scampering back to the imprisoned peacocks, but Charlie lagged behind. In a minute, Emma understood why. The old lady pinched his cheek and ruffled his hair, something Charlie absolutely hated.

But he endured her caress with good humor. Followed by Molly, who struggled for control of their guest's vast train, Lady Barbara went up the stairs. "Ta-ta! Until we meet again!"

"Who is she?" Emma whispered after a minute, too curious to be polite, though she was sure that Lady Barbara was well out of earshot.

"A retired actress. She married well but divorced badly and now makes the rounds of friends' houses. She and Mama were childhood playmates—they live near each other in London and attend the same church. Lady Barbara has become nearly as pious as my mother. I would rather she did not stay but I cannot turn her away."

"Of course not. But whatever will you do with the peacocks? It is raining very hard. We cannot just let them out upon the lawn," Emma said.

"We could roast them," Lord William said cheerfully. "I understand they were served as a delicacy at medieval banquets."

"No!" Caroline cried. Another unearthly shriek came forth from the basket. "You have upset them, Uncle."

"Oh, dear. Well, we cannot put them in the library. Nefret is in there. Peacocks need to roost, I believe. But we cannot put them in the chicken coop or the dovecote, they are too large. I have it—the wine cellar! There is no wine in it anyway."

Winkworth came around the corner, holding three of the smaller bags and trailed by a footman and the gardener, who held the others. "Very good, sir. I will move them in a moment."

"That is what I like about you, Winkworth. Your aplomb. You have more aplomb than anyone I have ever known."

"Thank you, sir."

Charlie gave over goggling at the peacocks and came to talk, his hands thrust into his pockets. "Do you really think we can keep them, Uncle William?"

"We have no choice, my boy. Lady Barbara likes to stay for several weeks."

Charlie nodded. "She visits us too—I mean, she visits Mama. Papa usually shuts himself in his study and locks it until she goes away. But she has never brought him any peacocks."

"He can count himself lucky," said Lord William. He went to the window, giving the wicker bas-

ket a wide berth, and looked out. It was indeed
raining heavily.

He touched a finger to the narrow framing of
the sash and it came away wet. Another leak. Was
there no end to the deterioration of this house?
He had no idea of how to pay for the repairs, given
that his last attempt at investing—he had bought
shares in a tobacco plantation in Virginia—literally
went up in smoke when the curing barns burned
down. The news had come in the morning's post,
and then Barbara had arrived with those blasted
birds.

Yet he felt oddly . . . calm. Almost . . . happy. He
looked over at Miss Snow, who looked altogether
fetching in that sunny yellow dress, and realized
that those feelings had something to do with her.

Perhaps it was true that love could mend a troubled heart. But, he reasoned, it could not mend
windows or roofs. He would have to find an heiress
sooner or later. Perhaps there was one wandering
about in the rain. He turned his back on his niece
and nephew and their pretty little governess and
went to the front door.

"Where are you going, Uncle?"

"For a walk. I need to think."

The children and Emma exchanged a look. "You
forgot your umbrella, Uncle William!" Caroline
ran up to him and found it in the umbrella stand.
"And you forgot to give me a kiss." The little girl
stood on tiptoe for one and Miss Snow gave him a
dazzling smile. His heart melted all over again.

Emma watched with the children as Winkworth
removed the complaining peacocks to the wine

cellar. He was followed by Mrs. Diggory, who carried a pan of shelled nuts and bread crumbs.

"Will they want this then?" she asked. "Are they like other birds?"

"They are birds of paradise, Mrs. Diggory," Charles said authoritatively.

"These are plain English walnuts. What do they eat in paradise?"

"We will look it up," said Emma. "Lord William's library has many books on birds. But remember, children, Nefret is not to be let out under any circumstances."

"She would not want to go out, Miss Snow. She hates rain. There is no rain in Egypt," Caroline said.

"There is a little, I think. But not very much. We can look that up too." Truly, a good library was a whole world unto itself.

She took the children by the hand and went with them upstairs. Charlie galloped—or tried to—but his sister was quite the little lady, placing her foot upon each step just so.

They entered the room with care, relieved to see that Nefret was curled up peacefully in a chair. Charlie went immediately to a shelf and pulled out Bewick's other book, *The History of British Birds*.

"Here, Caro. You can look at this. There are no peacocks but you will like the pictures."

Caroline took the book to the windowseat and began to read immediately. Emma reached for the globe upon the uppermost shelf, having decided to include a little geography along with the lesson on birds. "We shall find out where peacocks come from and everything else about them."

Charles nodded, eager to begin. Emma looked

for other, more scholarly works on birds and handed a few titles to him, not knowing whether he would find anything on peacocks.

She was glad that he was interested in the topic. Hours spent indoors on a rainy day could be dreadfully dull.

Emma looked through the windows and spotted the blurry figure of Lord William far down the road. He would be thoroughly drenched by lunchtime—perhaps he planned not to return. He had not seemed happy at the prospect of an extended visit from Lady Barbara.

Yet he had smiled at Emma most tenderly before walking out into the rain. He looked almost like . . . a man in love.

She put that ridiculous thought out of her mind and set out pencils and paper for the children's lesson.

CHAPTER 4

Three weeks later . . .

Lord William exited Cranley Hall through the French doors at the back, which he left open to the fresh air. In his hand was the morning post. There was a letter in his mother's handwriting to Lady Barbara, and one to him from his brother.

He tucked Lady Barbara's letter into his waistcoat pocket to give to her later.

She was still ensconced in the bedroom of her choice. Lady Barbara liked to sleep late. She claimed to be exhausting herself in the writing of a scandalous novel about her life upon the London stage. But she kept up her strength by arriving punctually for every meal, Lord William had noted.

He cast a baleful glance upon the peacock she had given him, which was perched in the low branches of a greengage plum, pecking at a withered fruit that no one had wanted.

He heartily wished they would fly away. Their

strange cries awakened him too often and the bad-tempered birds roosted where they pleased.

They were not even decorative. The peacock dragged his gorgeous tail about in the grass, refusing to show it, and the peahen, his drab little wife, was seldom seen at all.

But Cranley Hall was looking rather better. It still stood, to Lord William's relief. Perhaps he had been overly pessimistic. His recent investments were earning a respectable return, and he could even fix the roof, if nothing else, before winter. He might not have to marry a pug-faced heiress after all.

Of course, he still had Miss Snow to think about. His heart skipped a beat at the mere sight of her and his wayward mind spun tender fantasies of Emma, nestling in his arms . . . Emma, close enough to kiss . . . sweet Emma, laughing, chasing after the children, with her honey-colored hair tumbling down her back and her bonnet in her hand . . .

Emma, Emma, Emma! Damn the girl!

When she was not in sight, he could persuade himself that his feelings for her would last only as long as her stay at Cranley Hall. He might fancy her—might flirt with her—but at the end of summer she would be gone. Working on the house had proved to be a very effective distraction from her charms.

Fortunately, the children liked her so much they never left her side. Caro and Charlie were a great help in that regard. Lord William had no idea how much self-control he could summon if he were to find himself alone with Miss Snow.

He opened the envelope from his brother as he walked, removing a sheet of hieroglyphic writing that his sister-in-law had included for the children. He examined it, smiling. It was a clever mix of English letters and made-up Egyptian pictograms, rather like a rebus and easy to decipher.

Caro and Charlie would enjoy puzzling it out. Lord William tucked the hieroglyphic message in his pocket, next to his mother's missive to Lady Barbara, to give to them later. His niece and nephew had gone off to a neighboring farm, bright and early, with Miss Snow. He unfolded his brother's letter and began to read.

> *My dear William,*
> *We hope this missive finds you and the children well (if it finds you—the Egyptian post is most irregular). We wish that Caro and Charlie could share in our adventures——tell them the Sphinx sends her kindest regards. She is a mysterious old thing and no one knows the secrets she holds. The Great Pyramids await! We shall return in September. My fondest love to you, dear brother, and to the children. P.S. I hope that you have found Miss Snow's company agreeable. She is an intelligent girl and, we think, a treasure.*
> *Yr. aff'ct. brother, etc.*
> *Edward*

William sighed and folded up the letter. He was finding Miss Snow's company more and more agreeable as time went by. It was now full summer, yet her cheerful nature seemed never to wilt in the soaring temperatures, and she never ran out of things for the children to do.

They were often found in the library. She had

discovered books Lord William had no idea he possessed, taking many of the children's lessons from these.

Now that Nefret was past her heat, she had been let out of the library, of course. There was a limit to how long William would tolerate a smelly sand-box in his house, and he had reached it.

The library was a pleasant place to be once more. Miss Snow and the children had restored the shelves to perfect order, organizing titles first by subject and then by author.

They had reserved a small shelf for Nefret to nap upon. She was often in it, when not following Miss Snow and Caro about the house. His dear niece liked to spoil the cat with tidbits and carry her in a basket from place to place. The lazy cat was looking exceedingly well-fed these days.

Emma seemed to prefer holding Charlie's lessons out-of-doors whenever possible. The boy was learning a great deal about natural history and had moved on from there to a bit of chemistry and a dash of higher mathematics, which Lord William helped him with.

The imaginative Caro was writing and illustrating a book of her own, about a fairyland populated by cats and peacocks with human servants, in which everyone ate cake for breakfast, lunch, and dinner, and drank blue tea.

She had covered fifty pages on both sides in a childish but neat hand, and her fanciful pictures delighted all who saw them. Caro was not as clever at sums as she was at creative endeavors but she did her arithmetic anyway, to please her governess.

Miss Snow was indeed a treasure.

Lord William turned his steps toward the overgrown garden, where Jamie Crichton, the head gardener, awaited him. Head gardener was perhaps too grand a title—Jamie was the only gardener and newly hired. But if it pleased the old man to be called that, then Lord William did not mind.

Jamie Crichton had come highly recommended by another dear friend of Mama. The Baroness Bulwark had praised Mr. Crichton's horticultural expertise to the skies in a long letter—and she'd added that he was one of the few Scotsmen she could understand.

Lord William pondered his options as he walked.

He might have sufficient money to redo all the landscaping next spring, with a full staff under Jamie's command—or he might not. The books and treatises on gardening he'd had sent from London were full of interesting ideas. It occurred to him that if he bought fewer books, he would not be so damnably tempted to try new things.

He scarcely knew where to begin. But one had to start somewhere—anywhere—and do something, which was always better than nothing. This was Lord William's new motto, though he could not figure out how to translate it into Latin.

He wanted a riot of roses on this side of Cranley Hall, rambling over trellises and arbors. It was easy to imagine Miss Snow wandering within this fragrant enclave, a thought that pleased him very much. Every garden needed a resident goddess or nymph, and Lord William preferred the real kind to the marble ones.

At the moment, his newly planted roses were no more than crooked sticks set in rows, bravely unfurling a few green leaves. The trellises and arbors had not been built. Lord William's botanical dreams did not end there: he wanted laburnums, wisteria, rhododendrons and ferns . . . the list was endless and expensive.

Jamie, a more practical sort, had already dug the beds for a large kaleyard not too far from the kitchen. This much more useful garden would grow behind a screen of trees, lest a London guest be offended by the sight of humble herbs.

Lord William looked about. The overgrown acre looked much less daunting when viewed from the library windows. Here, down on the ground, the monstrous weeds were taller than he was. In the process of clearing the brush and brambles, Jamie had uncovered several small structures forgotten long ago, including a ramshackle shed and staved-in well house.

"Mr. Crichton? Are you there?"

"Aye."

"I can't see you."

A head-high clump of briars shifted to one side and there stood Jamie, one hand holding a scythe and the other, a shovel. His white hair blazed in the sun, matched only by the wonderful luxuriance of his white eyebrows.

It was difficult to tell how old he was, and Lord William had not asked when he hired the man. Though Jamie's body was slightly bent, he was powerfully built and compact. His eyes were a piercing blue, and seemed to see everything.

"Sir, we must cut this tangle awa' and rip out the roots. 'Tis good soil ye have, but it wants double digging."

"Of course. My thoughts exactly. Carry on, Mr. Crichton." Lord William had no idea what double digging was, but it certainly sounded like twice as much work.

"The farm lad has not come." The old man leaned on his shovel and looked meaningfully at Lord William.

"Dear me. We cannot wait indefinitely. The bare-root plants must be set in this morning."

"Aye, sir."

"The footmen are painting the outbuildings. I shall ask Robbie."

"The lad's gone to town with a list from Mrs. Diggory. A fine woman, she is."

"Indeed." Mrs. Diggory had supervised the planting of the kaleyard and Mr. Crichton had carried out her instructions to the last cabbage.

"A solid sort o' woman too," Jamie went on. "She'd keep a man warm at night, if ye ken my meaning, sir."

Lord William raised an eyebrow. "I believe I do. She is a widow, of course."

"Aye, sir." Jamie grinned.

Was a late-in-life romance blooming at Cranley Hall? Well, better late than never. William was pleased. A marriage between the housekeeper and head gardener would be a very good thing.

"About this double digging—I suppose I could help you."

" 'Tis verra hard work, sir."

"Still, it must be done." He took off his waistcoat and hung it on a dead branch, taking care to tuck the morning's letters deeper into the waistcoat pocket. Jamie, clad in a coarse cambric shirt splotched with mud, looked askance at Lord William's immaculate linen.

William sighed, stripped the shirt off and hung

it over his waistcoat. The warm air felt pleasant on his bare chest and he took a deep breath. Working together, they would clear the rest of the over-growth in no time. Jamie handed him the scythe and went back to his digging.

Whack. Whack. Briars and weeds were no match for a man who wanted to create a paradise.

Emma and Caroline had returned from their morning excursion and were removing their muddy shoes in the front hall.

The neighboring farm had fascinated Charles, who had lingered to talk to the farmer, promising to return to Cranley Hall for lunch. He seemed impressed by the well-fed, contented cows and the huge bull that had a pasture entirely to itself, and in love with the great draft horses that let him pat their shaggy coats and devoured his offering of carrots.

An immense, ginger-colored sow with a dozen piglets lined up at her teats proved almost as inter-esting. But the sow had been uneasy, glaring at them with beady eyes and issuing a piggy snort of warning when Charles got too close that made him jump back.

His sister preferred the chickens, throwing hand-fuls of corn to them with abandon, until the crowd of noisy fowl pecking around her feet necessitated her rescue by Miss Snow.

Mr. Keenan, the farmer, was a big-bellied, good-natured fellow with a loud voice. He answered all of Charlie's questions and invited them back.

Emma was weary. When Charles returned—and if the children could be persuaded to play quietly together for the rest of the afternoon—she could lie down upon the library sofa and relax with a good book. She hoped he would not be too distracted by the barnyard wonders. Charlie could disappear for hours when he was interested in something.

She was relieved to see the boy burst through the front door, full of enthusiasm about all he had seen on Mr. Keenan's farm. Emma listened patiently for a minute, then sent him and his sister to the kitchen.

Mrs. Diggory had promised them something good for lunch—probably cheese from the pantry shelf and a small plum tart apiece. These had been baked earlier in the week, when the greengages in the old orchard ripened, and pots of preserves put up as well.

The children ran down the stairs to the cellar kitchen, colliding with Winkworth, who was on his way up.

"Sorry, Wink!" That was Charlie's voice, fast receding. The boy must be famished.

The butler brushed off his immaculate coat as he reached the front hall. "Yes, Master Charles. Good afternoon, Miss Snow. Did you enjoy your visit to the farm?"

"We did. The children will take their lunch with Mrs. Diggory."

"And you?"

"Please ask Mrs. D. to send up a pot of tea and a light meal to the library. I shall be reading. Caro and Charlie may play in the adjoining room after they eat."

"Very good, miss."

She padded up the stairs, grateful for an hour

or two without the children, and opened the door to the library. The windows had been left open to catch the breeze, and the room was pleasantly airy, in contrast to the sultry warmth of the day. She might rest at her ease, though others were working hard—she heard the drowsy hum of bees and the new gardener thrashing in the garden below.

Nefret slumbered upon her shelf, so plump she almost did not fit. Emma reminded herself to ask the children not to give her so many treats. Their parents would be unhappy to see that the elegant Egyptian cat had made a pig of herself in their absence.

Emma went to the sofa, her favorite piece of furniture in the room. It was covered in threadbare velvet and had been made long enough for a tall man to stretch out upon. She had more than enough room for herself, a tea tray, and a book.

She sat and let down her hair, using her fingers to comb out the bits of straw and whatnot that blew about in the farmyard. Her hair still retained the warmth of the sun she had walked in; and it felt wonderful to air it out in the breeze from the open windows. She twirled it into a loose knot and pinned it back up on her head again.

Never mind reading. She would use her free hour to do nothing at all. A valuable experience, in her opinion. Doing nothing was most refreshing. That was when she got her best ideas, had her most amusing daydreams, and entertained wonderful romantic fantasies of whatever gentleman her young heart desired.

Lord William was the only gentleman she knew, of course. Curates did not count.

She reflected upon how interesting her life had

become since she had come to Cranley Hall. There was always something to do, unlike the unchanging routine of home, which revolved around her father's church and her mother's social circle.

Without sisters, brothers, or cousins, there were few opportunities for her to go outside the garden gate or even into the tiny village. Their neighbors were mostly elderly and content to stay at home. She had never been to a ball, never been to a dinner party, never traveled away from her home until the position with the Kents had been offered.

Nefret jumped down from her shelf a little awkwardly and came to sit by her. Emma sighed and stroked the cat's head. She did not see how she could be happy at home, having known a much livelier life here.

Even the scholarly Edward and Elizabeth were more interesting than her parents. And Lord William was positively fascinating.

She rested her head upon the back of the sofa and let the cat creep into her lap. "Oof! You have grown heavier, Nefret. No more bits of fish and sausage for you."

Her thoughts returned to Lord William. If she had to count up his good qualities, it would take the remainder of the hour she had to herself.

He had a great sense of fun and his niece and nephew adored him. He did not, as far as she knew, drink to excess or gamble, though both pastimes were *de rigueur* for gentlemen, according to her mother. He had a wonderful library and thought nothing of adding new volumes, no matter the cost. He did seem to be concerned about money where other things were concerned.

She wondered why. His income had to be many

times greater than what her family managed to live upon, but she supposed that the upkeep on so large a house ate up a great deal of it.

He seemed to be preoccupied with one repair project or another, especially lately. And he insisted upon his money's worth, often learning how things were done before he let a carpenter or plasterer touch the walls or windows of Cranley Hall. If work was not done to his satisfaction, he was wont to pick up tools and have a go at it himself.

Feeling a trifle naughty, Emma pondered some means of capturing his attention. He was always polite, always amusing, but always busy.

There had not been another picnic since the first. She could ask Mrs. Diggory and Bertha to prepare another hamper with his favorite foods—she knew what they were by now—and simply invite him to join her and the children.

It was not as if she could swing a hammer or climb a ladder. She supposed she could discuss his projects with him, though. That was safe enough.

His latest passion was gardening. His handsome nose had been buried in horticultural tomes and catalogues of perennial plants. The nursery-man's cart had rumbled up the drive several times with deliveries of shrubs and twiggy-looking things that supposedly would turn into roses.

Hence the new gardener, a dear old fellow with a slight Scots burr. Emma had been introduced to him by Mrs. Diggory. She had a feeling that the housekeeper liked Mr. Crichton very much, and was glad for her. Mrs. Diggory's five sons were scattered to the far corners of the British empire, and she missed them. Perhaps Mr. Crichton would provide companionship.

That was probably him in the garden outside the library windows, whacking away at the towering weeds and cursing in Gaelic. He was also cursing in English—no, that was Lord William's voice. Was the object of her reverie in the garden and was he working? A discreet peek outside was in order.

She tumbled the sleepy cat from her lap to the sofa, and padded over to the window. Oh—Emma suppressed a gasp when she saw him and shrank back behind the curtains.

He was naked to the waist, his smooth skin gleaming with sweat, and he was working very hard. She had never seen a man's bare chest and Lord William's was magnificent. His arms were hard and strong, his shoulders broad. He did not look like Lord Anybody at the moment, but like a man—the essence of a man.

Emma could not take her eyes away from him. He whacked and pulled at the overgrown plants, throwing each handful onto a pile at the side, clearing the earth for Jamie to dig.

He could not see her from this angle—but drat. Jamie Crichton could. The white-haired gardener moved into view and waved at her. "Good morning, lass!"

"Good morning, Mr. Crichton."

Lord William looked up, startled by the sound of her voice. "Hello, Miss Snow. Do forgive my, um, state of undress. There was nothing for it. Bareroot plants cannot be left in the sun."

"Quite all right." She smiled, hoping she sounded casual and not at all disconcerted by the sight of him without his shirt. Still, it would not do to stand there and gawk.

"What are you doing in the library?"

"Oh, just reading. The children will be coming up shortly."

Nefret jumped up on the windowsill beside her and teetered on the edge.

"Nefret! Do not jump down. It is too far and you are too fat." She reached for the cat. Nefret dug her claws into the windowsill and arched her back, not wanting to be picked up.

The gardener cast a canny eye upon the animal. "She is carryin' kittens, Miss Snow."

"What?"

"Stroke her sides, lass."

Emma did, feeling slight bulges she had not noticed before—but then she had little experience with cats and none whatsoever with kittens.

"Blimey!" Lord William said.

Jamie shrugged. "No need to swear in front of the young lady. Cats will be cats."

"Precisely my point," Lord William said. "We tried to keep the toms away when she was in heat, but Blimey got through our defenses."

"Och, you mean the innkeeper's great cat! I forgot his name was Blimey." Jamie laughed heartily.

Lord William threw down his scythe. "What will I tell Edward?"

"Who is Edward, sir?"

"My brother. He left Nefret with me. Blimey is a common tabby despite his enormous size, but she is a very unusual cat, of ancient pedigree and pure blood."

Jamie laughed again. "Is she, sir? Well, ye know the auld saying, I'm sure—at night all cats are gray."

"Thank you, Mr. Crichton. I will keep that in

mind," Lord William said crossly. "Would you like a kitten when they are weaned?"

"Certainly, sir. 'Tis lonely in the outbuildings and mice are aboot."

Lord William looked somewhat mollified. Emma stroked the cat again, still surprised at this turn of events. Kittens? Charles and Caroline would be wild with joy. She heard them enter the library and turned to face them.

"Children, we have a surprise for you. Or rather, Nefret has a surprise."

"Has she caught a mouse? She does that all the time," Charles said, looking bored.

"No. She is going to have kittens."

"Kittens! My dream came true!" Caroline cried.

CHAPTER 5

A few minutes later, Caroline sat upon the library sofa with Nefret in her lap, petting her with utmost tenderness. Her brother settled for reading the encyclopedia entry on cats to discover how long it might take for the kittens to be born. He sat upon the floor with the heavy book cradled in his crossed legs.

"I did dream of kittens, Miss Snow," Caroline said.

"Of course, my dear," Emma said absent-mindedly.

"I wonder whether they will look like Blimey or Nefret," Charles said.

"We shall see," Emma said. She was still a bit awestruck—not by the revelation of Nefret's pregnancy but by her unexpected glimpse of Lord William without his shirt. It would not do to go back to the window and look at him again, but that was exactly what she wanted to do.

However, a sensible person did not give in to

such impulses. Nefret might follow her animal instincts, being an animal, but Emma could not.

She noted that the purring, plump cat looked altogether content. Cats were lucky creatures. Though Nefret would bear Blimey's kittens, she did not have to marry her rather disreputable lover and no one really thought the worse of her.

A resounding knock interrupted Emma's thoughts.

"Tra la! May I come in?" asked Lady Barbara. She did not wait for a reply but sailed into the room, trailing yards of rustling silk as usual. "My dear child," she said to Caroline. "You must not allow that cat to sit upon the sofa."

"She is in my lap," Caroline replied. The little girl circled a protective arm around her pet.

"Nefret is going to have kittens, Lady Barbara," said Charles.

Lady Barbara let out a little shriek. "Now? Here?"

"No," said Emma. "Charles, have you found out the information?"

"It says that the gestation period of *Felis catus*, the domestic cat, is sixty-five days. But we do not know precisely when Blimey done the deed." He looked up from the thick book.

"Good gracious! Such vulgar language, Charlie!" Lady Barbara shot him a lofty look. "And who is Blimey, if I may ask?"

"He is the innkeeper's cat," said Emma. "Perhaps you saw him when you passed through Cranley. He has but one eye and one ear, and no tail."

"He's fought with all the village dogs," Charles said. "And he always wins. He has stripes and he walks with a swagger. He's the biggest cat for miles and miles."

"Perhaps I did see him," Lady Barbara said. "Of course, my carriage was only hired and the driver did not stop long at the inn. But I do seem to remember a large and very ugly striped cat sunning itself in the inn yard."

"That's Blimey," Charles said with pride. He closed the encyclopedia and got to his feet, taking the spot beside his sister on the sofa before Lady Barbara could.

"Charles," Emma said reprovingly. "You must make sure that our guest is comfortably seated first."

The boy got up again and offered his place on the sofa to Lady Barbara with a wave of his hand.

"Oh, dear me, no," she said. "I am not fond of cats. I will sit here, in the armchair." She settled herself and her trailing skirts within it, and studied Caroline for a moment.

"What shall you do with the kittens, my dear?" Lady Barbara inquired.

"Keep them all," Caroline replied without a moment's hesitation.

"You cannot," Lady Barbara said. "You see, there will be more and more kittens if you do. Cranley Hall will be overrun eventually."

"I don't understand," Caroline said.

Lady Barbara took a deep breath and looked to Emma. "Miss Snow, do you wish to explain further or shall I?"

Emma managed not to laugh out loud and she could see Charles hiding a smile. "Do continue, Lady Barbara."

"Very well." The old lady turned to Caroline, undaunted by the child's expression of innocent confusion. "You see, darling, the great Creator of us all gave His creatures the ability to continue His great work upon this earth. They can reproduce at will and save God the trouble."

"Oh," said Caroline politely, seeming more interested in the cat than the fine points of theology.

"To accomplish this, God gave His creatures the gift of love. I am sure that Nefret loves Blimey very much. And Blimey loves Nefret."

"Very, very much," Charles said under his breath.

Emma shut him up with a killing glare.

"Will they love their little kittens too?" Caroline asked.

"Yes, dear," Lady Barbara said. "Nefret will take excellent care of them. But Blimey—um—has done his part."

"So why will there be too many kittens at Cranley Hall?"

Lady Barbara seemed to be at a loss for words.

"Well, perhaps that will not happen," Emma said briskly. "We do not need to worry about it now, Caroline."

Lady Barbara nodded and rose from her chair. "Well said, Miss Snow. Would you mind if I closed the window? The breeze has grown too warm."

"If you close the window, the room will be even warmer," Charles pointed out. "That is a scientific fact."

"You must think of her comfort and not science, Charles," Emma said. She motioned the boy to the window that he might close it, but Lady Barbara got there first. She reached out to draw the windows in, saw Lord William, and called to him. "Willy! You are out-of-doors without a shirt! It is hardly respectable!"

"The day is hot," he replied curtly. Emma imagined his scowl.

"I can see that, Willy dear. Dear me—you are perspiring. You look like a common laborer, my boy."

"There is no one else to do the work," Lord William called back.

Emma found the sound of his deep voice, however cross, positively thrilling. It warmed her through and through. Inside the coolness of the library, she could not blame the sun for that agreeable sensation.

"Hallo, milady!" That was Jamie.

Lady Barbara did not even bother to respond to the gardener, turning away from the window with an expression of faint disgust, muttering, "Willy seems to have forgotten that he is a gentleman. I must write to his mother."

Emma scarcely knew what to say. Lord William had been most kind to Lady Barbara, considering how the old lady was imposing upon him. In Emma's opinion, their uninvited guest thought rather too well of herself.

Suddenly a great commotion arose outside. Piggy grunts and squeals came from the garden, mixed with the sound of branches cracking and men scrambling to safety.

Emma and Charlie rushed to the window and looked out. The ginger-colored sow from Mr. Keenan's farm stamped upon the cleared earth, shaking her heavy head, bent upon mayhem.

"Damnation!"

" 'Tis a pig!"

"I can see that, Jamie." Lord William got up on

the brush pile but sank in up to his knees, struggling to keep his balance.

"Ye're nae safe there!" Jamie took refuge behind a tumbledown shed. "Look sharp! She is comin' after ye, milord!"

"No, Jamie—watch your back! She is coming after you!"

The sow charged and stopped before the shed, grunting.

"Oh, do be careful, sir!" Emma called. By this time, Caroline had squeezed between her brother and Emma to look out. Lady Barbara stayed in the background, wringing her hands and running to and fro.

"Uncle William! That is Farmer Keenan's pig!" Caroline called.

Lord William glanced at his nephew for a fraction of a second but returned his gaze to the angry sow. "Charlie, do you have something to do with this?"

"N-no," Charles said, not meeting Emma's eyes. "We saw the pig and her piglets but—"

His hesitant reply was interrupted by another loud squeal from the pig, which swerved around the shed and headed toward the back of the house.

"Charlie!" Lord William called. "Why is the pig here?" He waded out of the brush pile, stepping over the tangle of leafy branches. "Tell the truth!"

"She's headin' for th' kaleyard!" Jamie brandished his shovel like a spear. "We must ketch her afore she tramples th' wee cabbages!"

"Damn the wee cabbages! What if she gets into the house? The French doors are open—I came through them."

The two men galloped around the corner of the

house, out of sight. Charlie rushed out the door of the library, followed by his sister, who dragged Emma by the hand. Lady Barbara, still fluttering and wringing her hands, brought up the rear of the pell-mell parade.

They halted at the top of the stairs.

At the bottom was the sow, skidding to a stop upon the marble tiles. The animal peered about, her snout twitching this way and that.

"Farmer Keenan said that pigs are highly intelligent, Miss Snow," Charlie began. He seemed quite nonchalant about the sow's presence, unlike his sister, who clung to Emma's skirts.

"This is no time for a lesson in natural history," Emma said sternly. "What have you done, Charles? Why has the pig come here?"

"It is looking for something, mark my words," said Lady Barbara, peering over the balustrade. The pig looked up at the sound of her querulous voice and grunted. "Dear me. What a strange noise."

"What does the pig want, Miss Snow?" Caroline peeped out from Emma's skirts but would not let go.

"I have no idea," said Charles.

Emma knew him well enough to distrust his innocent tone and wide eyes. The pig fixed its beady eyes upon the boy and wiggled its snout, as if trying to get a whiff of his smell. "Charlie, you must tell the truth!"

Lord William and Jamie entered the hall through the French doors, walking softly and armed with shovels to head off the pig. He had put his shirt back on but it was not tucked in, giving him a ruffianly air quite suitable for the task at hand.

"Do not hurt her, Uncle!" cried the soft-hearted Caroline.

"She is more likely to hurt us, Caro," he replied.

"Aye," said Jamie. His thick white eyebrows drew together and he scowled fiercely at the sow. She seemed unimpressed.

Mrs. Diggory chose that moment to come up from the kitchen, and shrank back at the top of those stairs, her eyes wide with fear. The sow took a few steps in her direction.

"Fear not, Mrs. Diggory!" Jamie waved his shovel wildly. The sow took refuge behind the wide base of a marble pillar.

Mrs. Diggory put a hand upon her heaving bosom and gasped for breath. "Thank you, Mr. Crichton! Oh my! Oh my!"

"Take heart, dear lady," the gardener said gallantly. "Ye have brave men t' protect ye!"

Lord William threw him an annoyed look. "Do not play the conquering hero, Crichton. We haven't caught it yet."

All eyes were on the pillar's base. But they could see only the twitching snout. Then the rest of the animal suddenly appeared, its trotters clicking on the marble as it looked about.

They held their breath.

The sow made a break for freedom. She charged toward the French doors, between the two men, who jumped apart.

Lady Barbara shrieked and clutched the balustrade as if to keep from fainting. Emma, knowing they were in no immediate danger at the top of the stairs but not knowing whether pigs could climb stairs, drew the children to her just in case.

The sow streaked past in a blur, through the

doors and outside the house. Jamie followed, cursing in Gaelic again. "Ye shall not gie in th' kale-yard! Get back!"

Mrs. Diggory let out a sigh of relief but stayed where she was. Winkworth stood behind her now, and a gaggle of maids, and Bertha, waving a rolling pin.

"She wants her piglet!" Bertha called. "Saw the little beast with me own eyes, outside, rootin' fer scraps in the midden. Nice and fat, it were."

"Piglet?" Lord William asked. "What piglet? When did this household acquire a piglet?"

"I had nuffink to do with it!" Bertha growled. "'Twere that boy, you may be sure!"

"Charlie!"

"Master Charles!"

"Charles!"

"Oh, brother dear . . ."

Charlie looked at each of his accusers in turn. "Well—I bought a piglet from Mr. Keenan with my pocket money. And I had it in the house for a little while—the sow is smelling where it went. I let it outside, but only for a few minutes, because I wanted lunch. I will give it back, if it is this much trouble."

"Indeed you will. How—and where—did you plan to keep it?" Lord William set his shovel aside and put his hands on his hips, glaring up at his nephew. "We have no sty."

The boy seemed chagrined. "I didn't think about that. I was going to build a pen from rocks. I didn't know its mother would come for it."

"Och! Back, ye great beast! Back, I say!" came Jamie's gruff shout.

Lord William dashed outside to assist him.

"Winkworth!" Emma called. "Please find the footmen! The sow and her piglet must be caught and returned to the farm!"

The butler edged around Mrs. Diggory and ran to the French doors, which he shut and bolted, pushing a potted palm against them for good measure.

Emma and the children came downstairs to look out from the glass, while the butler went out the front door to find help. Lady Barbara left, eager to return to the safety of her bedchamber.

The pursuit and eventual capture of both sow and piglet took the better part of an hour, as the creatures relished their freedom. Indeed, they seemed to positively enjoy leading everyone in a breathless chase.

Brought over from his farm by a footman, Mr. Keenan and his swineherd hatched a plan. The swineherd threw himself upon the squealing piglet—Emma immediately reassured Caroline that it had not been harmed—and simply waited for its mother to come after it. The other men tiptoed up, holding a net.

Would it be strong enough? It was meant for keeping birds out of the fruit trees, not holding pigs.

The sow let out a loud *wheee*, and charged.

"Cracking!" Charles said gleefully, though he was immediately silenced by a look from his governess. At a signal from Lord William, the men tossed the net over the sow. It struck out with its trotters and squealed angrily, until the swineherd reached into his pocket and pulled out a wrinkly old turnip, feeding it to her through the net.

The sow chewed the turnip thoughtfully, looking a trifle winded. The piglet sat down on its plump rump beside her, glancing up expectantly, as if hoping its mother would share this treat. She did not.

Caroline sighed happily. "May we keep the dear little pig, Miss Snow? It will be no trouble."

"No. It will not stay little."

"Mr. Keenan said it would be a right big un someday." Charles frowned, now that the excitement was over. "I wonder what Uncle will say. I suppose there will be consequences."

Lord William, who had gone around the house and come in the front without them hearing him, dusted off his breeches and spoke. "Indeed. Whatever were you thinking, Charles?"

The boy hung his head. "I don't know."

William nodded. "Exactly what I expected you to say."

"I thought you might like a piglet for your birthday, sir," Charles said suddenly.

"A likely story."

"Well, it was what I would want for my birthday. But I am sorry to have caused so much trouble, Uncle."

Lord William crossed his arms over his chest and grinned. "You have your choice of penances, my boy. You can muck out the stables or help the footmen finish painting the outbuildings. Better yet, you can help Mr. Crichton clear brush from the garden."

"Yes, sir."

"He is too old for the pursuit of pigs and he deserves a rest from his exertions, don't you think?"

"Yes, sir."

"I will fetch some cold lemonade for him, sir,"

said Mrs. Diggory. She turned to go down the stairs, speaking to the maids. "Come along, girls. Don't stand there gaping. There is always work to do."

Lord William nodded. "Thank you, Mrs. Diggory. Heed her words, Charlie. You will have to work harder than anyone to make up for this escapade."

His expression was grave but Emma, who was watching him carefully, saw the twinkle in his eye if Charles did not.

"My dear nephew, I have half a mind not to let you go to the Berryfield Fair this year."

The boy looked truly repentant now. "Oh, no, sir. I will help Mr. Crichton as you said—and do all the other things too."

"We shall see. The fair is two weeks away. By the way, Mr. Keenan returned your pocket money. He assured me that you paid a fair price for the piglet."

"I will put the money into the church poorbox," Charles said manfully.

Lord William laughed. "Very good. The poor will welcome your contribution and it will keep you from buying any more animals for a little while."

"Then may I go to the fair, Uncle?" he said hopefully.

"Perhaps," was all that Lord William would say.

CHAPTER 6

Two weeks later . . .

The first day of the Berryfield Fair dawned bright and clear. Nearly all who lived at Cranley Hall, upstairs and downstairs, would go. The senior servants were coming and going in the front hall, attending to last-minute preparations while Lord William, the children, and Miss Snow breakfasted.

Mrs. Diggory was bringing up empty baskets from the kitchen that would soon be filled with her purchases at the fair. But one basket held pots to be mended at the tinker's stall and that one clanked. "I hope these will all fit into the cart, Mr. Crichton."

"I will see to it, Mrs. Diggory." The white-haired gardener picked up three baskets in each hand and went out the door that Winkworth held open. The butler, who was also going to the fair, was dressed in his Sunday best, which did not escape Mr. Crichton's notice. "Ye're quite the gent, Winkie. Looking for a lass, are ye?"

Winkworth did not deign to answer this question.

"Hoity-toity," the gardener said over his shoulder, setting the baskets by the cart in the drive.

Charles dashed out, wiping crumbs from his mouth. "Mr. Crichton! May I ride with you?"

"Aye. If ye behave, ye can drive the horses where the road is flat."

"Hurrah! Caro will be jealous. She will have to sit in back."

Jamie shook his head. "Nae. The little lass shall ride in th' carriage with Miss Snow and th' master."

Mrs. Diggory came out to see that the cart was loaded properly. "Mind the cat, Mr. Crichton! She might jump into a basket and stow away."

The gardener looked down. Nefret had ventured from the house to see what all the commotion was about. She sniffed at the baskets and wandered off again, her bulging middle now quite obvious.

"Aye, Mrs. Diggory. She is already thinkin' about a nest."

"Do you mean to say that cats nest in trees, Mr. Crichton?" Charles asked. "How curious!"

"Nae, lad. But cats keep their kittens in unlikely places. She will hide her little ones well when they come."

Caroline came out next, looking worried. "Where is Nefret? She must stay at home."

"She went that way, miss." The gardener pointed and Caroline scampered off to find her pet.

"Caroline!" Miss Snow came out the front door, followed by Lord William, who went to the carriage and looked at the harnessed horses. She looked about for her charge. "Caroline! Do not run away!"

The little girl reappeared, holding Nefret with some difficulty.

"I think perhaps that you should not pick her up now, Caroline." Emma took the pregnant cat from her with care, setting her down inside the front hall and returning to stand outdoors.

"Very good. Let us depart," Lord William said.

"We are ready—is Lady Barbara coming?" the housekeeper asked.

"No," William said. "She let us know that she attends only the most elegant entertainments. Fairs are beneath her, or so she says."

The rest of the party came out, chattering eagerly, and waving good-bye grandly to the few servants who chose not to attend. Some clambered up into the cart and those who preferred to walk set off down the road, talking among themselves about the great day ahead. One of the waiting carriage horses whickered, and stamped its hooves.

Lord William handed Miss Snow into the carriage first and then picked up Caroline. "Come, little princess! To the fair!"

First the cart and then the carriage pulled up at the top of the hill to let the stragglers catch up. The passengers craned their necks to see the striped tents with banners at their topmost points and the brightly painted gypsy wagons in the valley below. The sprawling fairgrounds were bordered on one side by a meandering river, and Lord William could just see the silvery thread of the brook near his house that fed it.

The walkways between the tents were already crowded. People came from all over Devon to the Berryfield Fair, to see and be seen by all who attended, from the gentry to the humblest folk of the countryside.

And they came to buy and sell animals—there were hundreds in the pens—and to buy fruits and vegetables, and all sorts of household goods.

Emma heard the faint sound of a hurdy-gurdy from the fairground. There would be the usual popular entertainments: acrobats and waxworks and fortunetellers, and a sideshow, of course. And booths with catchpenny trinkets, ribbons and other pretty things for girls, and slingshots and toy pistols for boys—and games of chance to separate yokels from what little money they had.

She turned to Lord William and smiled at him. He smiled back.

"I do love a fair, sir."

"As do I, Miss Snow. I hope that you will allow me to demonstrate my uncommon throwing skill at the booths. I shall claim a prize for you, Caro."

"I want a doll!"

He looked down at the little girl nestled between him and her governess. "You shall have it, one way or another."

He signaled to the coachman and the group from Cranley Hall continued down the hill to the fair.

Lord William and Miss Snow strolled through the fairground at their leisure, the party from Cranley Hall having dispersed in several directions. Charles had elected to go with Mr. Crichton to look at what he found most interesting: flocks of sheep and the like.

Caroline stayed with her governess and her uncle, taking first Lord William's hand and then Emma's, and sometimes being swung between them. The little girl wanted to stop at every stall and examine the merchandise, exclaiming over gaudy ribbons and paste jewelry as if such things were priceless treasures.

They came to the part of the fair where still greater illusions were purveyed: machines that tested manly strength and wonders of the world sculpted in wax, shown to all comers at a penny a peep.

A strapping yeoman took up an immense hammer, ready to slam it down upon a platform rigged to a ten-foot tower. A giggling girl waited to one side to see if he could ring the bell at the top of the tower.

"May we watch?" asked Caroline eagerly.

"Of course," said Lord William.

The yeoman lifted the hammer high above his head with both hands and brought it down with great force. But the bell did not ring.

"Ye can do better," called the showman. "Ha'penny a hit. Try again!"

The yeoman's girl dug in her handbasket and produced a small coin. "Come on, Clancy! Make me proud!"

Clancy's face turned red. He waited for the showman to accept the ha'penny and picked up the hammer again. This time he took a deep breath, swung with all his might and just managed to ring the bell.

His girl applauded as the showman cried his

praises. Clancy turned a deeper shade of red but seemed quite pleased with himself. He wandered off, arm in arm with his girl, who listened eagerly to his explanation of why he had not been able to ring the bell the first time.

"Uncle, do you think you could do that?" Caroline asked, her eyes glowing with excitement.

"Of course not."

"But you are very strong—stronger than Clancy."

"That brute? Perhaps not, Caro."

The little girl tugged at his hand. "Please, Uncle. You could try. Just for fun."

"Ha'penny a hit," the showman intoned, his thumbs under his braces, walking up and down in front of his machine.

Lord William looked askance at the hammer leaning against the platform, and then at Emma. Was she hiding a smile? Ought he to make a fool of himself? He had no chance whatsoever of ringing that damned bell. The powerfully built yeoman could not do it on his first try, and barely managed it on his second.

"Please please please," Caroline begged.

"Very well. I will try." He gave the showman a coin from his pocket and picked up the hammer. Emma and Caroline stood back.

Lord William held the hammer over his head. It seemed oddly light. Had his work in the garden added strength to his grip?

"One moment, sir!" The showman ducked behind the machine and Lord William set down the hammer. "Allow me—I ha'just the machinery between customers—tighten a screw or two—there."

A small crowd gathered while the showman fiddled.

No doubt the man knew they would, William thought. What rustic Hercules would not enjoy seeing a lord test himself against this infernal machine?

He looked up at the bell. The ten-foot tower that supported it seemed to have grown higher. More onlookers joined the crowd. Miss Snow and Caroline stayed at the forefront. Lord William could not very well back down now. He swung the hammer over his head and brought it down—hard.

The bell emitted an ear-splitting clang and everyone cheered loudly. The farmers and laborers jostled each other to be next, and a few who knew him took the liberty of slapping him upon the back.

Emma beamed at him. "Oh, well done, Lord William!"

He shrugged, not wanting to seem too pleased with himself, and took Caroline's hand. She tugged him down to give him a congratulatory kiss that made him laugh. He had a sneaking suspicion that the platform was rigged. The amiable showman knew exactly how to draw a crowd and he, Lord William, had been no more than bait.

"Step up, step up! Ha'penny a hit! You first—the brawny fella!" The showman handed the hammer to his next customer, and tipped his hat to William. "Thank'ee kindly, sir!"

They walked on.

Charlie ran up to them, spilling sweets from the paper cone he held. "I want to see the waxworks—they are educational, Miss Snow! Heroes of England and all that." He did not mention the more gruesome tableaux, thinking that she would not allow him to go.

"Caro, do you want to see them?" Lord William asked.

"No, Uncle. I don't like waxworks. I hate the way they stare."

"Very well. Charlie, you may go. Have you spent the money I gave you?"

"Almost, sir."

"Here is more." He dug in his pocket and dredged up a handful of coins.

"Uncle William rang the bell with his hammer, Charlie." Caroline pointed to the showman and the tower. "He is stronger than anybody."

"Really? May I try?" the boy asked.

"No, my boy," Lord William said. "There are more amusing ways to waste money."

"Well, the waxworks then." Charles scampered off and the three of them walked on.

The people who came to the fair were as entertaining as the exhibits and amusements. Gentlemen, though not many ladies, mingled freely with country people and village shopkeepers, joined here and there by a stray soldier on furlough and doxies with painted faces.

They came to a tent bedecked with paper stars and moons. The placard before it advertised the services of a fortuneteller who could be glimpsed within, swathed in shawls and strings of beads, and wearing a wobbly turban atop her head.

"Miss Snow, would you like to know what the future holds?"

"I do not believe in such nonsense, Lord William," she answered lightly.

"Oh, she has a crystal ball," Caroline exclaimed.

"There—on her table. Can she see things in it, Miss Snow?"

Emma smiled. "She can see a customer coming." A farm woman walked in front of them, pulled back the half-open curtains of the tent and sat down at the fortuneteller's table.

A tinny melody in a minor key began to play from some hidden machine inside the tent. Caroline seemed awed. "The sign says she is a Gypsy Seeress from the mysterious East."

Lord William laughed. "Yes—the mysterious East End of London. She comes to the Berryfield Fair every year, Caro. And she is no more a Gypsy than I."

"How do you know, Uncle?"

"She told my fortune when I was young"—he peered inside the tent as discreetly as he could—"yes, she seems to be the same woman."

"But that was a long time ago. You are very old now."

"I am not that old, Caro." Lord William looked pained and Emma had to laugh.

"Tell me what she said," the little girl persisted.

"Oh, the usual. I got my shilling's worth. That I would grow up—and travel abroad—and marry someday."

"Who are you going to marry, Uncle William?"

The memory of that day came back to him with sudden clarity. The fortuneteller had said simply that he would marry a country girl with honey-colored hair and sweet ways, and let it go at that. Yet the vague description did fit Emma.

Lord William looked directly at her. Was their meeting an act of fate or an ordinary coincidence? Did it matter which? If his niece were not hanging onto his hand, he would tell Miss Snow of the fortuneteller's prediction. But he said nothing.

She did not look away, startled by what she saw in his eyes—tender emotion that had not been there a moment ago and a spark of amusement that disconcerted her. Surely she was imagining things. She turned to the little girl and spoke gently.

"Caroline, that is enough. Do not ask so many questions."

"But if Uncle marries, then I will have cousins."

Emma stroked the child's hair, hoping to distract her. "Perhaps you will someday. But no one can foretell the future."

Caroline seemed to accept that answer, looking around for new delights. Fortunately, they were near the enclosures where the cattle and smaller creatures were kept.

Those who came to buy looked them over from their side of the fence, while the sellers touted the merits of their animals in no uncertain terms.

Emma spotted Mr. Keenan. The farmer was presiding over a pen holding ginger-colored pigs very like his wayward sow in appearance and addressing those who stopped to listen in a very loud voice.

"Fine, fat Tamworths, gentlemen. The very best Ginger Tamworths. Magnificent specimens. Not often found in these parts—oh, dear. Here is Lord William. How're ye keepin', sir?" Keenan doffed his cloth cap and made an awkward bow.

"Very well, thank you."

"I am sorry about the sow, sir, as I said."

"No harm done."

"I sent a lad over with rashers for yer table, to make amends."

Lord William nodded. "Mrs. Diggory mentioned it. Thank you."

"How is the little pig?" Caroline asked maternally.

"He's grown much bigger in two weeks, miss. Don't suppose you would recognize him now."

She peeped over the side of the pen and pointed. "There he is. His tail is especially curly. You should tie a ribbon on it, Mr. Keenan."

The farmer seemed surprised. "That is him. Well, sir, I don't suppose you are interested—"

Lord William interrupted. "No. We do not want a pet pig, with or without a ribbon on its tail. Thank you, Mr. Keenan."

They moved on, walking nearer to the nurseryman's cart and the rows of pots his wife had arranged in neat rows around it. "Good day, sir! Good day, milady!" the man called. "Here are yer old favorites, climbing roses and the like. And exotic varieties for a touch of the tropics. D'ye keep a greenhouse, sir?"

William's quick glance told him that the man had exactly the plants he was looking for and a few he had never seen. He would stick to the old favorites. The transaction could be quickly completed and his purchase delivered when the fair was over.

"Ah! A horticultural wonderland, Miss Snow!"

Emma looked and saw only straggling shrubs that did not look wonderful at all. To each his own, she thought. She could go elsewhere with Caroline, who was tugging at Lord William's sleeve.

"Caro, what is it?"

"There is Mrs. Diggory and Mr. Crichton." She

pointed. "May I go with them? I don't want to look at plants."

Lord William saw his housekeeper and gardener looking at a display of kitchenware, having just left the pots to be mended at the tinker's open-air stall.

"Yes, if Miss Snow would be so good as to take you. There is your brother, Caro." He grinned at the sight of Charlie gawking at the rough-looking tinker, who was making fascinating sparks and a great mess with solder as he chatted up the housewives waiting in line with their pots.

"I shall join you shortly, Miss Snow."

"Yes, my lord."

Emma and Caroline went hand in hand to the tinker's stall, where the little girl ran up to her brother. Charles turned away from the show of sparks with a sigh as Jamie and Mrs. Diggory came over to him.

"I should like to be a tinker," the boy declared.

"Bite yer tongue or yer wish might come true, lad. Tinkerin' is no life for a gentleman," Jamie said severely. "And furthermore—"

But Charlie dashed off to the next tent before he heard the rest. The group from Cranley Hall followed, ducking through the canvas flaps after him. Charles was pointing to a sign painted in scarlet and canary yellow.

SEE TRELAWNY'S FAMOUS TYGER!
A RATTER OF RENOWN, ALSO KNOWN AS
THE DEVON TERRIR

"The spelling is wrong," Charlie whispered. "The last word has only two r's, I believe."

"Ye may be right," Jamie said, winking at Emma. "But no one 'ere cares. Besides our Miss Snow, that is."

Below the sign was Blimey, lolling on a scarlet cushion, looking massively bored and hardly terrifying. David Trelawny came up to greet them, jovial as always.

"What will it be? Ale fer ye, Jamie? Lemonade for the ladies?" The innkeeper doffed his hat and made a very grand bow. "Ah, here is his lordship, come to look at the cat. Good day, sir."

"Davy, you are shameless!" Lord William said, laughing.

"Thought Blimey might attract custom to the inn, m'lud. People remember 'im!"

The boisterous group of laborers drinking Davy's beer raised their mugs in an impromptu toast. "Here's to the owld cat! Long may his tail wave!"

"What there is of it," added a little fellow, wiping the foam from his upper lip. The men erupted into guffaws.

"Blimey has much to answer for, Davy," Lord William said. "He has sedu—"—he looked down at Caroline—"ah—he has befriended our cat."

"She had no one to play with," Caroline explained. "But she will soon have lots of kittens."

"You don't say!" Susie, the innkeeper's daughter, wiped her hands on her apron and came over. "He got away from me that day. But he came home soon enough, m'lud. I had no idea—"

A ploughman at the table bellowed for more beer.

"Shut yer gob! I am talking to the quality!" she yelled back.

"Back to work, Susie," her father said. "Hoi! Here is Mr. Winkworth. Care for a pint, sir?"

Winkworth, who had just ducked in under the open side of the tent, nodded to Davy and to Lord William. "The day is warm. I believe I will."

Lord William went into his pocket again and tossed a few coins upon the table. "Allow me, Wink. Enjoy it."

"Thank you, sir." The butler looked surprised but turned to talk to Susie, who favored him with a dimpled smile, ignoring the man who had bellowed at her.

"Could I stay with Mrs. Diggory?" Caroline pleaded. "You walk too fast and I want some pie and lemonade."

"We will have to go to another tent for pie," the housekeeper said. "But it is no trouble, sir."

"I'll carry ye, lassie!" Mr. Crichton picked up the little girl and set her on one shoulder. "How is that?"

"I can almost reach the top of the tent!" Caroline stretched up her arms to the striped canvas.

"Mind that you don't bring it down," the housekeeper said mildly. "Come along, Jamie. I would like a bite to eat meself."

"Aye, Mary Diggory. Lead and the little lass and I shall follow."

Lord William and Emma exchanged a look. "Good-bye!" she called. Caroline waved, proud to be high above the crowd.

So it was first names now between his new gardener and the housekeeper, Lord William thought bemusedly, and he was not the only moonstruck fellow at the fair. Was moonstruck the right word?

Perhaps the strong summer sun had simply addled his brain.

They left the tent after telling Charlie to stay near Mr. Winkworth and not wander off without saying where he was going. Susie gave the boy a glass of cool water and let him pet Blimey, who accepted the attention with a yawn. Susie continued to talk to the butler, her chin in her hands and her elbows on the counter. Her father saw to the customers.

"Well, everyone seems happy enough, Miss Snow. Are you enjoying yourself?" Lord William asked.

"Very much."

They walked back toward the cattle enclosures again, where he engaged a few of the farmers briefly in conversation, then returned to her side.

"I was thinking of cattle-raising, Miss Snow. There are gentleman farmers who have made a handsome profit from it, when it is done on a large scale. I cannot rely solely on the income from my investments and the yearly rent from our tenants just barely covers expenses at Cranley Hall."

He seemed lost in thought for a moment. Emma was delighted that he talked to her so easily of such things, as if she were his lady wife and not just governess to his niece and nephew. But she put that pretty fantasy firmly out of her mind as he continued to talk.

"I have no experience with such matters and books are no substitute for what these men know. What do you think, Miss Snow? Should I buy beeves or sheep?" He sighed.

"I have not the least idea, Lord William. My father is a vicar. He leads a very different flock."

He grinned. "Well said, Miss Snow."

"Thank you, sir."

"Shall we walk on? Perhaps we will find a shady spot where you may rest—it is cooler near the river. I fear that I have dragged you from one end of Berryfield Fair to the other."

"I am sure we have not seen it all." She was not tired, though it was past noon and she had not eaten since breakfast.

"Are you hungry, Miss Snow? Please say yes. There is the pieman's tent!"

"Yes, yes, yes."

"A most diplomatic answer. We shall get along splendidly if you insist upon agreeing with everything I do and say." He hastened with her to the pieman.

"I would not go that far, Lord William," she laughed.

He held up the tent flap for her to enter. The pieman's wife gave them a broad smile. "Hallo! What may I give ye?"

"We would like two apple pies—those little ones that we can eat out of hand. And cider if you have some—and is that a ham? Two slices of that, cut very neatly, for a lady's lunch."

"Yes, sir. It is a ham, sir." She set about preparing the food he ordered as they watched and putting it on wooden plates. The cider was served in mugs that the pieman's wife took down from a rack. At least no other customers had used them very recently, Emma thought.

They sat down at a table by themselves. Lord William took out a penknife to cut the thick slices of trimmed ham down to size. It was very good ham but she was determined to be dainty, even in this rustic setting.

"You eat no more than a mouse, Miss Snow. Will you not have more?"

"Oh, yes. This mouse is very hungry."

She soon finished her food and Lord William went back for more. The cheery informality of the colorful tent under which they sat and the hubbub of the great fair all around them did wonders for her appetite.

If her parents saw her now, they might very well be shocked. The Right Reverend Mr. Snow and Mrs. Snow were not the sort of people who attended country fairs—at least her father did not. But her mother had, once upon a time, or so Emma seemed to remember her saying.

Perhaps, as a girl, her mother had even danced. She saw a stage not far away where a group of fiddlers began to play a country air with more enthusiasm than skill. Sturdy farm lads and apple-cheeked girls came up the rough stairs upon one side to join hands in the dance.

She watched them, wishing that she did not have to be so exceedingly respectable at all times. What fun it would be to step lightly and weave in and out as they did, under poles decorated with ribbons and summer flowers.

"Do you dance, Miss Snow?" Lord William asked softly.

"I wish I could," she replied. "But I have scarcely had the chance."

"There is a ballroom at Cranley Hall, you know."

"There is?" She looked at him with astonishment. "Where? I have never seen it. How could I miss so large a room? I have been everywhere in the house."

Lord William laughed. "I did not know you were so curious, Miss Snow."

She blushed, wishing she had not said so much. "Forgive me."

"Quite all right. Had I known you wanted to dance, I would have shown you the ballroom. But it is in a sorry state. The plaster roof is falling down and the parquetry floor is in disrepair."

"But where is it, sir? You still have not told me."

"It is not part of the house, but if you go out the back and walk a little distance to the north, you will see a round structure behind the lime trees. The walls and windows are completely covered with ivy."

"Oh!" she exclaimed. "Do you mean that giant green beehivey thing?"

"Yes."

"I had no idea it was a ballroom."

He looked a little sad. "It has not been used for fifty years or more. But perhaps we shall someday."

Emma looked longingly at the dancers on the stage, who had finished their frolic and were about to begin another. "I hope so."

He looked at her thoughtfully. "Well, how shall we amuse ourselves now? Mrs. Diggory and Jamie have Caroline, and I suppose Winkworth will keep an eye on Charlie."

"He seemed to have his eye on Susan Trelawny," Emma said, smiling.

Lord William nodded. "Good. Wink is far too serious. She is a very friendly girl. I suppose an innkeeper's daughter would have to be." He stopped himself. "I mean nothing wrong by that, Miss Snow. She is perfectly respectable, of course."

"Of course."

Miss Snow's smile was demure but he sensed the restlessness behind her own perfect respectability. Full of pie and ham, he was ready for an afternoon adventure himself. Perhaps it was time to throw caution to the winds and do something he had never done at the Berryfield Fair.

If Miss Snow was willing, they could do it together.

He motioned to the lazy little river that meandered on its way not far from the pieman's tent. "Would you like to drift upon the river, Miss Snow? A rowboat can be hired for a few pennies. It is a pleasant way to while away an afternoon."

"Yes," she said eagerly. "I should like that very much. But I have never been in a boat."

"There is a first time for everything."

"Indeed." She gave Lord William a dazzling smile. This was the first time they would be alone together, without a child or an unexpected guest or anyone else to interrupt them. What a wonderful thought.

CHAPTER 7

"Excellent, Miss Snow! Let me see about hiring the boat—and if you would purchase two more pies and perhaps some cheese, we shall want for nothing. Meet me by the river."

He put money on the table, rose before she could change her mind, and dashed down to the water's edge.

Emma shook her head. She hoped he knew what he was doing. She knew nothing about boats and even less about swimming.

Of course, it was not as if they were sailing away on a clipper ship or a fearsome man-o'-war. She had seen such vessels only in books. The rowboats down at the dock looked comfortingly round and cozy, rather like pudding tins.

She walked back to the counter and asked the pieman's wife to wrap up two more little pies and a large piece of cheddar in the clean handkerchief she gave her. Then she walked down to the river.

Emma was glad to see that the water was shallow

and slow-flowing, coursing between curved banks and overhanging trees to which a small boat could be easily tied.

Other rowboats were already out upon the river, manned by single men and a few couples. The men's sleeves were rolled up—the better to display their muscular forearms and rowing technique, no doubt—and most of the women let one hand trail in the cool water.

They looked blissful.

She walked to the floating dock and inspected the rowboats tied to it.

"What do you think?" Lord William asked. "This one is ours. His Majesty's navy boasts none finer."

The rowboat was newly painted in blue and white, with seats of polished wood, and oars stowed diagonally through the oarlocks.

"It looks quite, er, shipshape."

The boatman smiled. "Thank'ee, miss. You will 'ave a grand time."

Lord William stepped from the dock into the boat and stood in its middle, balancing against its slight rocking. "Come, Miss Snow." He reached out to take her hand. He too had rolled up his sleeves to above the elbow.

His hand was warm and his strong grip banished her momentary nervousness. Emma stepped down into the rowboat as if she had done it a thousand times before and sat down in the bow, spreading her skirts and tucking her feet under the seat. She kept the food wrapped in the handkerchief upon her lap.

"Ye're as pretty as a picture, miss."

She did not mind the boatman's easy familiarity and smiled up at him and then across at Lord

William, who had taken his seat. He grasped the oar handles, sliding the oars back through the locks, and waited for the boatman to untie them.

The man fiddled with the knotted rope and stood up, holding the tarred end. "Ready, sir?"

"Yes."

The boatman threw the rope into the boat and pushed them away from the dock with a long pole. Lord William began to row.

He did know what he was doing. His rhythm was steady, an easy push-and-pull motion that moved the little craft out to the middle of the river in no time.

The river seemed larger than it had from the shore, but not so large that she was frightened.

"Where did you learn to row, my lord?"

"Oh, here and there. It is something boys just do, I suppose, like swimming. I have taught Charlie to swim."

"He is an adventurous boy, and I suppose his mother did not mind."

"No. Elizabeth is fearless herself. Quite the opposite of my own dear mama. *She* was convinced I would drown if I so much as walked through a puddle—she never knew that I waded in the brook all the time, just like Charlie. It leads into this river, you know." He pointed upstream. "In that direction."

Imagining Lord William as a boy in rolled-up breeches, with muddy feet, was not difficult at all. Emma smiled.

"Mama would never let me take out a boat at the fair," he continued.

Emma gave him a questioning look. "Really? Then how—"

"A friend's family had a boathouse on the river not too far from here. He taught me. I have always liked it."

Another boat went past. The man rowing it huffed and puffed, making noisy splashes with the oars and trying unsuccessfully not to circle to the right.

Emma waved. The other man nearly lost his grip upon one oar, regained it with difficulty, and resumed going in circles but to the left.

"Poor fellow. He will run aground in no time."

They lost sight of the other man when his boat went around a bend. A happy couple passed them. The clever oarsman had figured out how to hold a girl and row a boat at the same time, and he gave Lord William a very smug smile.

Sooner than Emma had thought possible, they had reached a much prettier stretch of the river. How was it that women were not permitted to learn so useful a skill as rowing? The mere thought of the afternoons she had spent in feminine pastimes like embroidery or simply listening to her mother's endless chatter seemed irksome by comparison.

Lord William pulled the oars out of the water and rested for a moment, letting the slow current move them onward.

"I wish I could row."

"It takes more strength than I think you possess, Miss Snow. You might capsize the boat. No, no—all you need do is trail your hand in the water and look pretty."

"I see. I suppose I can manage that." She leaned over the side and looked down into the water. "I see a fish. What is it thinking, I wonder?"

"I could not say. The thoughts of fish are beyond knowing."

Emma laughed as Lord William admired her graceful form and merry smile. Her round bosom showed a little as she leaned over more to put her hand in the water. Was there ever a figurehead so lovely? He counted himself a lucky man indeed to have seen Miss Snow like this.

He began to row again, with a steady power that moved them smoothly down the river. Emma sat up, fascinated with the back-and-forth motion of the oars and their noiseless dips under water that curved over the blades with each stroke.

The man who wielded them was no less fascinating. She felt again as she had the day she glimpsed him in the garden: here was the essence of a man.

Alone—well, somewhat alone—with Lord William upon the tranquil water of this little river was where Emma wanted to be and all that she wanted in the world at this moment. The happy clamor of the fair seemed very far away, though she could still see the colorful tents and the throngs of people milling about.

"Where shall we go, Miss Snow?"

"Wherever you like."

"That is a rash statement. I cannot take you out of sight of everyone without risking your reputation."

"I shall not tell a soul. Row on!"

He began to row rather faster and less smoothly. "We must return."

She pouted. "Why?"

"Do not play the coquette. It does not suit you. You are young and—and inexperienced. And you live under my roof, and you are my niece and nephew's governess, and my brother would have my head if I so much as kissed you."

"But I would like very much to be kissed," she said wistfully. "By you," she added after a moment's thought.

"I consider myself honored," he said dryly.

She sat up even straighter. "I suppose you think I am too forward."

"I scarcely know what to think. You have put me in a very awkward position."

She opened the handkerchief and took out a pie, biting into it without tasting it. Lord William was being entirely too decent. She did not know what to do besides eat.

"Miss Snow, perhaps we can compromise. If you would like to stay out upon the water and watch the fireworks from here, where we are not alone, I would agree to do so."

Her eyes opened wide. "I did not know there would be fireworks tonight. Here? So far away in the country?"

"Fireworks are shipped like any other commodity," he said. "Though I would rather not be on the boat that brings them, given how easily they explode. Have you never seen any?"

"No. This is a great day for first experiences, my lord. My first boat trip. My first fireworks. My first . . ." She bit her lip.

Had she been about to say *first kiss*? Well, she would not have that from him. At least, not now. Not here. He was firm in his resolve, knowing that he was doing the right thing by an innocent girl.

Lord William looked around to make sure there were other people in other boats nearby. He turned back to see her take another absent-minded bite from the pie in her hand. She was not looking at him.

A crumb of pastry fell down her bodice. She moistened her fingertip with her tongue, reached down her bodice to get the crumb, and licked it off her finger.

Just jump overboard, you fool, he told himself silently. *Pray that the water is cold.*

She looked up at him at last. "Nightfall is hours away," she said, taking another bite of pie.

"Two hours, perhaps less. The sun is beginning to set."

"Then you have time to teach me to row."

He looked at her doubtfully. "We would have to change places."

She stood up.

"Please sit down!"

She took a step toward him. "We cannot change places if I do."

"You will unbalance the boat!"

She took another step.

"Miss Snow!"

"Here I come."

A ripple from a passing craft made the rowboat rock. She toppled into his lap.

"Damnation!"

"Why are you cursing?"

"I cannot very well manage two oars and an armful of warm girl."

She giggled. "But you row with such skill."

"Shut up, Miss Snow."

Oars first, or they would be lost. He had to let her stay upon his lap while he slid the handles back through the oarlocks and pointed the blades up.

"Is that to keep from losing the oars? I remember you doing that at the dock."

"Yes. But you must get up—only not all the way up at once. Move slowly and carefully, if you please. And then return to your seat."

"I don't want to—but I will," she sighed.

Damn the girl. She stood up facing him, brushing crumbs from her dress. He clutched the seat and thought of—things he ought not to think of. Her closeness and her impertinence were equally intoxicating.

"Why will you not teach me to row?"

"I have a feeling we will both end up in the water."

She looked toward the boatman, who was waving.

"We are close to shore."

"Miss Snow, the water is as wet by the banks as it is in the middle. Surely you proved that to your satisfaction when you and the children ended up in the brook."

She laughed. "I suppose you are right."

"You would not wish to be drenched again. Therefore, sit down." Emma did not. William was utterly exasperated but unable to make any sudden moves.

"My lord, if you stand up—slowly and carefully, as I did—we can still trade places," she pleaded. "You can give me further directions from the bow. It is called the bow, is it not, Lord William?"

He gritted his teeth. "It is. But I have no intention of opening a nautical academy for silly little governesses who do not listen and who will not obey."

"Dear me. Aye, aye, I'm sure. Please accept my apologies, Captain Bligh!"

"You are impossible. Sit down."

Another ripple in the current forced her to do just that. Next to him. With her beautifully rounded thigh pressing warmly against his.

He drew in a long breath, counted to ten, sang a stanza of "God Save The King," and observed a moment of silence, in that order, until he was calm.

"Are you feeling all right, Lord William?"

"Quite all right, thank you. Very well. I will teach you to row. Grasp the handle of the oar, Miss Snow."

She grasped it with both hands.

He wrapped one strong arm around her and put one hand over her two. "Pull back." She tried but he did most of the work for her.

"That was easy," she said proudly.

He took his hand away. "Lean into the bow, let the oar go forward over the water, dip it in, and pull back again."

She bent almost double. The oar she held chopped at the water on her return pull, dragging and splashing. The boat began to turn in a circle. "Oh, dear. I suppose I must practice," she said cheerfully.

"You do not have to lean so far forward. Slow and steady. Back and forth. Try again."

And she did. She rowed in circles and in straight lines, with his help and without, until her hands were sore. She tried rowing with both oars while he moved to her seat and ate the cheese and the other pie. If she wanted to row so badly, by God he would let her.

To her credit, she would not give up. But at last she opened her hands to show him the beginning of a blister. "I can do no more today. Thank you for teaching me, Lord William."

He was shocked—and angry with himself for not thinking that she might be injured. "Why did you not tell me that your hands hurt, Miss Snow?"

"You would have made me stop," she said simply.

"Ah. You do not like to be told to stop any more than you like to be told what to do," he said.

"No," she admitted. "Oh, look!" A brilliant shower of stars burst open over the darkening sky. "The first firework! Ah, it is lovely!" She wetted the handkerchief in the water and wrapped it around her sore hand, looking up in wonder.

A second firework, a crimson streak of light, pierced the heavens and exploded into more stars. "Oh! Ah!" Her lips parted and her eyes glowed.

Dear God. Lord William reminded himself that she had tried his patience, tested his resolve, and tempted him beyond belief. But he could not resist her at that moment.

He leaned forward and kissed her full on the lips.

Emma rocked back on her seat and gasped. "Oh! I liked that better than fireworks!"

He kissed her again. And again.

CHAPTER 8

Two weeks later . . .

Lord William hacked away the last of the briars. He and Jamie had made great progress, and a considerable pile of brush. The stableboy and a few of his friends would drag it all away to the top of the hill. It would make a magnificent bonfire, come the end of October, on All Hallows' Eve.

He pulled out a handkerchief and mopped his brow. Let the village lads be scratched by the thorns and broken branches. He had had enough. Anyone who considered gardening a gentlemanly pastime had obviously never done it.

Jamie came round the corner of the house, trundling an enormous wooden wheelbarrow filled with the plants Lord William had purchased at the fair. They had been kept in an improvised shelter since being delivered after the fair's end, but they could wait no longer.

"More plants, sir. Now why on airth did ye buy so many? Ye cannot eat 'em."

"The nursery-man let me have them at half-price."

"Half price? Th' robber was chargin' double in th' first place," Jamie grumbled.

Lord William simply shrugged. He was not about to explain to Mr. Crichton that he hoped to propose to Miss Snow next summer, right here in his glorious garden, which was not looking very glorious at the moment. He hoped the flowers and roses would cooperate.

Miss Snow knew nothing of his scheme, of course.

He had fallen madly in love with her on the night of the fair—and he had been avoiding her since. After much thought, he deeply regretted kissing her during the fireworks and thought it best to apologize for his ungentlemanly conduct.

Oddly, Miss Snow had seemed uninterested in his apology. She did not seem to be avoiding *him* and contrived to encounter him at every opportunity. It was a good thing Cranley Hall had so many rooms and long corridors—he could hear her coming.

Dear girl. No matter what she thought, he should not have permitted himself such liberties. He was steadfast in his determination to keep his distance, just in case one or both of them came to their senses. Though he lacked experience in matters of the heart, according to his libertine papa, Lord William did not want to rush into anything.

He watched Jamie unload the plants and set them

out in the beds, thinking over the logical progression of his planned courtship.

His brother and sister-in-law would return from Egypt sometime in autumn, and the children would go back to their home. So would Miss Snow—and Lord William would have all the time in the world to woo her, without the impropriety of doing so while she lived under his roof.

True, her village was some distance away from Cranley Hall, but by fortunate coincidence, it was not far from the country house of a dear friend, who was, happily, always in London.

Lord William could stay at Mixton Grange for as long as he liked . . . and . . . and . . . it would all work out very nicely.

His plans were somewhat vague but his willpower was great. Above all, he wanted to do things the right way. As he had never courted anyone and certainly not proposed, he would have to figure out how to go about it on his own.

He would not imperil Miss Snow's reputation with another impulsive kiss or a romantic rendezvous— her innocence was at stake. She was young. He could wait.

"What is this, m'lud?" Jamie took a strange little plant from the wheelbarrow and cast a wary eye upon its spiky leaves.

"Ah! That is a rarity, Mr. Crichton. It is a pineapple."

"Good God. It will nae grow in England." The old gardener put it on the ground rather quickly, as if he thought it might bite him.

"Find a warm spot for it with plenty of sun."

"Oh, aye. Next to th' coconut tree and th' dancin' monkeys? Ye are mad, sir."

Take a Trip Back to the Romantic Regency Era of the Early 1800's

4 FREE BOOKS ARE YOURS!

4 FREE
Zebra Regency Romances!
(A $19.96 VALUE!)

Plus You'll Save Every Month With Convenient Home Delivery!

We'd Like to Invite You to Subscribe to Zebra's Regency Romance Book Club and Send You 4 Free Books as Your Introduction! (Worth $19.96!)

If you're a Regency lover, imagine the joy of getting 4 FREE Zebra Regency Romances and then the chance to have these lovely stories delivered to your home each month at the lowest price available! Well, that's our offer to you and here's how you benefit by becoming a Regency Romance subscriber:

- *4 FREE Introductory Regency Romances are delivered to your doorstep (you only pay for shipping & handling)*
- *4 BRAND NEW Regencies are then delivered each month (usually before they're available in bookstores)*
- *Subscribers save almost $4.00 off the cover price every month*
- *You also receive a FREE monthly newsletter, which features author profiles, discounts, subscriber benefits, book previews and more*
- *There's no risks or obligations…in other words, you can cancel whenever you wish with no questions asked*

Join the thousands of readers who enjoy the savings and convenience offered to Regency Romance subscribers. After your initial introductory shipment, you'll receive 4 brand-new Zebra Regency Romances each month to examine for 10 days. Then, if you decide to keep the books, you pay the preferred subscriber's price, plus shipping and handling.

It's a no-lose proposition, so return the FREE BOOK CERTIFICATE today!

Say Yes to 4 Free Books!

Complete and return the order card to receive your FREE books, a $19.96 value!

4 **FREE BOOKS** are waiting for you! Just mail in the certificate below!

FREE BOOK CERTIFICATE

YES! Please rush me 4 FREE Zebra Regency Romances (I only pay $1.99 for shipping and handling).I understand that each month thereafter I will be able to preview 4 brand-new Regency Romances FREE for 10 days. Then, if I should decide to keep them, I will pay the money-saving preferred subscriber's price for all 4... (that's a savings of 20% off the retail price), plus shipping and handling. I may return any shipment within 10 days and owe nothing, and I may cancel this subscription at any time.

Name _____

Address _____ Apt._____

City _____ State_____ Zip_____

Telephone (____) _____

Signature _____

(If under 18, parent or guardian must sign)

Offer limited to one per household and not to current subscribers. Terms, offer and prices subject to change. Orders subject to acceptance by Regency Romance Book Club. Offer Valid in the U.S. only.

RN084A

If the certificate is missing below, write to:

Regency Romance Book Club,

P.O. Box 5214,

Clifton, NJ 07015-5214

or call TOLL-FREE 1-800-770-1963

Visit our website at www.kensingtonbooks.com

Treat yourself to 4 FREE Regency Romances!
A $19.96 VALUE... FREE!
No obligation to buy anything ever!

REGENCY ROMANCE BOOK CLUB
Zebra Home Subscription Service, Inc.
P.O. Box 5214
Clifton NJ 07015-5214

PLACE
STAMP
HERE

Jamie left the stubby, spiky plant where it was and walked off muttering under his breath.

Lord William sighed. He would have to plant it himself. He had thought of building a glassed-in greenhouse, even a fashionable *orangerie,* and had learned from his latest delivery of books how such structures were built. The expense was staggering and certainly not worth it for a puny pineapple or two.

Foolishly, he had imagined himself presenting the fruit to Miss Snow when the nursery-man had talked him into buying the pineapple plant. She would undoubtedly prefer sweetly scented roses.

Which he would give her, heaps of them, by the wheelbarrow. This garden was for her, and like his secret love for her, it would put down roots as the seasons came and went and burst into fullest bloom before next summer.

He picked up his precious pineapple and set off to find a place in the sun for it.

Charlie sat on the dusty floor of the attic. He had promised his little sister that they would play until the time came for their afternoon lessons.

He did enjoy the game, even if Caroline had invented it. It was called, very simply, Egypt, and the rules could be changed the moment either of them got bored.

She sauntered about in a flowing garment made from old linen tea towels, her crown of peacock feathers and gold tinsel worn slightly askew. He studied the sign his sister was dusting with a corner of her front tea towel. There seemed to be no doubt as to who was in charge.

CAROLINE (MISS PHARAOH)
QUEENE OF THE UPER & LOWR NILE
& THE BITS IN-BETWEEN
BOW DOWN!

"Very good, Caro," he said admiringly.

"Miss Snow has been helping me with my letters."

Nearby, Nefret reclined at her ease upon a velvet cushion purloined from the drawing room reserved for visitors of especial importance. As there had been none for some time, the housekeeper was not likely to notice the absence of the cushion for a while.

Hitching up the tea towel around her middle, Caroline placed a small bowl of cream by the cushion.

"How did you get that all the way up here?"

"You forgot to bow down."

Charlie obliged and bowed. "You didn't answer my question."

"I don't have to. I am the queen. Anyway, I didn't spill a drop."

Nefret, who had grown quite a bit larger around the middle, got up from her cushion with some difficulty. She sniffed at the cream and took a few laps of it, just to be polite.

"Good kitty. You must keep up your strength," Caroline said solicitously.

Charlie stroked the cat with utmost gentleness. She purred and settled back onto her cushion. "How many kittens d'you suppose she'll have, Caro?"

"Lots, I hope." Caroline sat down and began to fashion herself a scepter out of a short wooden pole and a paper star. After a few minutes, she waved it at her brother. "Behold! This means I have great powers!"

Charles sighed. "If you are queen, Caro, then who am I?"

"You are my slave. You have nothing. And you can only eat onions. No roast beef. No pudding."

He shuddered. "I hate onions."

"No exceptions."

"I suppose I need a costume."

Caroline nodded with queenly indifference as Charles got up and went over to the old trunk that was their hidden source for such things. He rummaged through it, coming up with a shabby frock coat.

It had once been bedecked with floral embroidery and tiny glass beads, which had mostly fallen off. The coat looked rather moth-eaten now, but its faded glory appealed to the boy.

"Could I be your grand vizier instead of a slave?" He held up the coat for his sister's inspection.

"What do they do?"

"I think they poison people. And rub their hands and scheme against the king."

Caroline thought it over. "Well, since I am not a king, I suppose you can be a vizzy-whats-it."

Charles put on the old frock coat. Its tails dragged upon the floor and raised small clouds of dust. Nefret sneezed.

"Be careful, Charlie. If she sneezes too much, she might have the kittens too soon."

He picked up the tails and went to admire himself in the cracked looking glass. "Do you know, Caro, this must be Grandpapa's coat. He is wearing one very like it in the portrait in the hall."

Caroline came over to inspect it more closely.

"It must be hundreds of years old. Grandpapa was never young."

Charles laughed. "He must have been once. I wonder if we will see him again." He strutted and preened in the shabby old coat, still holding up the tails. "Do you think he is ever coming back from Paris? I asked Uncle William and he said no."

His sister shook her head. "Paris is very far away. Almost as far away as Egypt." Her lower lip began to tremble. "I miss Mama and Papa. Are they ever coming back, Charlie?"

He gave her an affectionate hug. "Of course. Didn't Mama say so in her letter? Do you have it?"

He had succeeded in distracting her from crying, he noted with pleasure. She ran to where she had hidden the hieroglyphic letter—under Nefret's royal cushion—and pulled it out without disturbing the cat.

"Read it to me, Charlie," she said in a tremulous voice. Then, remembering that she was a royal personage with a scepter to prove it, she added, "I command you, my vizzy."

"Yes, my queen. I believe the grand vizier actually does open the letters, when he is not poisoning people." He unfolded the missive carefully. Caroline had looked at it hundreds of times since its arrival, and memorized the message that Charlie had translated.

But he was happy to read the letter again, allowing his sister to lean against his shoulder while he pointed out the funny little pictograms and rebus symbols that his mother had invented just for them, knowing her clever children would enjoy such a puzzle.

She sent all her love, told them of the wonders to be seen in the fabled Valley of Kings, and how odd it was to ride upon a camel and live in a tent. Papa had added a few lines in his neat hand, saying that Charlie and Caro might come along on the next trip, if Mrs. Bumpus could be persuaded to join the caravan.

Charlie made a face. He hated Mrs. Bumpus much more than he hated onions. Was there no way that Miss Snow could stay forever and ever?

"Caroline," he said suddenly. "You are a girl and you know about certain things—"

"What things?" said Caroline absently.

"Love. Things like that."

She gave him a doubtful look. "What are you talking about, Charlie?"

"Do you think that Uncle loves Miss Snow?"

"I don't know."

"What if they married?"

"How romantic," Caroline breathed, her eyes wide.

"If Miss Snow became our aunt, then Mrs. Bumpus would have to go and live with her older sister. She used to say she would, don't you remember?"

"Ye-es," Caroline said slowly. "But we are not staying at Cranley Hall for always and always. Mama and Papa are coming back—you said they would."

Charles thought it over. "And Mrs. Bumpus will come back from Bath."

Caroline shook her head. "She cannot go to her sister. Her sister lives very far away. In the South Seas."

"What is she doing there?"

"She is a missionary. Or a pearl diver. Something like that."

The children sat in companionable silence for a moment, with nothing more to do than watch the fine dust drift through the sunlight. Caroline spoke first. "Charlie, let's not play Egypt. Let's play South Seas instead."

"All right, then. But I get to be a pearl diver wresting treasures from monstrous clams."

"So long as I am queen!" said Caroline.

The afternoon was seasonably warm, though the sun had not yet reached to where Mrs. Diggory and Jamie Crichton were sitting. They were not far from the kaleyard, resting briefly from their endless labors upon an old stone bench and keeping a dignified distance between them.

"He is mad, I tell ye," growled Jamie.

"Now, now. Lord William is only pursuing a passion. Many gentlemen have taken up gardening, I understand."

The old man shook his head. "Pineapples! I ask you! Mary Diggory, I hae seen only one afore and that was in th' Edinburgh consairvatory where I learned ma trade."

Mrs. Diggory seemed impressed. "I did not know you worked in a conservatory, Jamie."

"Aye, I did, for many years. It was a fine place, all of glass and near as big as Cranley Hall. Then I worked for Lady Bulwark, bless her diamond buttons. 'Twas she who recommended me so highly to his lordship, the madman."

His tone was almost merry and the housekeeper

smiled to hear it. "And so we met. You must thank her ladyship for me."

"She is too grand for thankin', Mary. But I am grateful to her th' same as you."

The sun reached the old couple at last, and they sat for some minutes more, enjoying its warmth.

"May I ask ye something?" Jamie began, edging a little toward her.

She edged the same distance away. "Yes?"

"My dearest Mrs. Diggory—the time has come to tell ye that—och! Words fail me."

She gave him a coy look.

"Lass, are ye thinkin' what I'm thinkin'?"

"Certainly not," she replied briskly. "Not that I know what it is you are thinking. I am a respectable widow."

He sat very straight, looking cross all over again. "I was only goin' to ask if ye might return my feelings, woman. I had a daft notion of marryin' ye."

"Oh! Mr. Crichton, that is very different. I will think it over."

"Much obliged," he said.

Emma and Lady Barbara were waiting for their tea in the drawing room but Winkworth had not appeared. The clock upon the mantel had struck the hour with a musical chime and subsided into relentless ticking.

Really, Emma thought, she should be with the children. The time set aside for their afternoon lesson had been frittered away in aimless talk with Lady Barbara on the subject of her memoirs. The old actress seemed to love having an audience once more and she simply would not stop.

But Emma did not want to be rude. When Winkworth came in with the tea tray, she would ask him to find Caroline and Charlie, and then make her escape.

How unfortunate that Lady Barbara seemed to plan on staying at Cranley Hall indefinitely. Perhaps that was why Lord William had been well-nigh invisible in the last two weeks.

The memory of his kisses still thrilled her. She was able to recall the moments that led up to them in every detail. Their silly squabble in the hired boat. Her insistence upon learning to row. His patient instruction, and the way his arm had moved around her to demonstrate the proper technique. And she had compared him to Captain Bligh! He had not seemed to mind—not very much, anyway.

Lord William was not avoiding her. That was simply not possible. No, his eyes were filled with a tender light—dare she call it the look of love?—on those rare instances when they met by chance. He was simply waiting for a moment when they could be alone.

Alas, between the children and Lady Barbara, the moment had not come in the last two weeks.

That august personage had rustled into the drawing room not an hour ago as Emma was writing a letter, settled herself into a chair and sunk alarmingly low. She had heaved herself out, noticing that a cushion was missing.

"Dear me! This chair is a deadly trap! I might have been severely injured!"

Emma had managed to seem concerned and assisted Lady Barbara to another chair. No doubt Caroline and Charles had made off with the cushion, but where it was now was anyone's guess.

Lady Barbara yawned very wide. "Miss Snow, could you fetch me a book of poetry? Any poet will do. Do you know, I just thought of writing my memoir in verse instead. It would be quicker."

"Perhaps," Emma murmured.

"I shall study the masters. Whom do you recommend?"

"Ah—let me look." Emma rose from the desk and went to a handsome bookcase inlaid with mother-of-pearl. It held slim volumes with highly decorative bindings and there might be a poet or two upon its shelves, though most of Lord William's books were in his library, where they belonged.

Winkworth knocked and entered with the tea tray. Lady Barbara fluttered and cooed. "Tea! The very thing. How wonderfully restorative. We shall drink our tea and then chat some more, shall we not, Miss Snow? Did you find a book of poetry? Please look again. What a pleasant way to while away the afternoon!"

What a pleasant way to waste everybody's time, Emma thought uncharitably. "Mr. Winkworth, have you seen Caroline or Charlie?"

He made her a slight bow. "Yes, miss. They came into the kitchen just as I was leaving. Charlie told the cook that diving made him hungry. Or something like that."

"Has he been swimming? He should not go alone."

"No, Miss Snow. They were in the attic, dressing in old clothes and playing at make-believe. He was pretending to be a pearl diver, though he wore an old coat that dragged on the floor. Not quite the thing for undersea exploration, miss."

Emma had to admire him for keeping a straight face.

The butler continued. "Miss Caroline told us she was a queen—and that Nefret, her royal pet, needed a morsel or two as well, so as not to starve."

Emma smiled. Caroline's affection for the cat knew no bounds.

"Dear Nefret!" crowed Lady Barbara. "And how is our mother-to-be, Winkie?"

"The animal is well, ma'am. She has grown exceedingly round. The cook has prepared a bed of straw for her by the hearth."

"Excellent. Precisely what I would have recommended," Lady Barbara said.

Emma looked at her with mild surprise. The old lady did not care for cats. She had complained of Nefret's presence often enough, perhaps worried that the Egyptian cat or Blimey would attack her precious peacocks.

But it had not happened. Nefret's increasing girth made it difficult for her to move as swiftly and silently as she once did, and the mighty Blimey had retreated to the village. The silly birds were well able to defend themselves, in any case, screaming and swooping about.

Lady Barbara waved a beringed hand at the butler. "Thank you, Winkie."

He frowned and left.

"Now, Emma dear, as I was saying . . ."

Emma was not listening. Her mind was on Lord William and their first magical kiss under the exploding fireworks. Then she thought about their second kiss. And their third.

She wanted more.

CHAPTER 9

At the end of August . . .

"That cat is restless, Mrs. Diggory, and you know what that means. But she won't go near the nest what I made. Ungrateful, I say." The cook patted the straw and gave Nefret an encouraging smile. "Here, kitty kitty. Come in and lie down. Nice clean straw, it is. Just for you."

The housekeeper pondered the matter while Nefret looked on, meowing softly. Her belly heaved, preparing for birth.

"Perhaps the straw is too scratchy," Mrs. Diggory said at last. "Let us make her another one, with soft rags, in a quieter place."

"Hmf! Too good for a cat, if you ask me," Bertha said.

"Has she not rid the kitchen of mice?"

"Yes, I s'pose she has. But I was saving them rags."

Mrs. Diggory nodded. "Good. We need them. Where are they, Bertha?"

"The cat needs them, you mean." The cook reached behind the heavy oaken door of the kitchen for her ragbag.

Mrs. Diggory reached into it and took out a handful, stuffing it into a different basket that was wider and easier for the cat to climb into. She added more rags, until the basket was thickly padded and set it in a quieter corner of the kitchen, away from the hearth and its clangor of pots and pans and cooking sounds.

Nefret got in rather awkwardly and curled up as best she could. The new basket seemed to satisfy her.

"There. That will do, Bertha."

"Well, I never," said the cook. "So much fuss for a cat. I am off to bed then."

"I will stay."

"Servin' as midwife, Mrs. Diggory?"

"Yes."

"Ye have a soft heart."

The housekeeper did not reply, but brought a chair over to sit beside the nervous cat.

Much later that night, four tiny kittens came into the world. Nefret got through each birth with scarcely a cry. She gave each kitten a thorough going-over with her rough tongue, despite their squirming and infinitesimal peeps of protest. When all were born, Nefret lay down and nudged them into position for their first meal.

Curled around her newborns, the purring cat seemed well pleased with herself. Mrs. Diggory, overwhelmed with weary joy, put her head down on her crossed arms and fell fast asleep at the kitchen table.

* * *

"Caro! Caro, wake up! The maid said there are kittens in the kitchen! Nefret had four!"

Caroline sat bolt upright, her eyes wide open though she looked as if she was still dreaming. "Four?"

Charlie bolted out the bedroom door and his barefoot sister quickly followed, looking this way and that for him, but he had disappeared. Once at the top of the landing, she collided with Emma, awakened by the commotion. "Miss Snow! There you are!" The little girl rushed pell-mell past her down the stairs.

"What is it, Caroline?" Emma asked sleepily, tying the sash of her *robe de chambre* around her waist.

"Kittens!" the little girl cried. "Come and see!"

"Oh, my!" said Emma, flying after her down the stairs. She was not decently dressed but no one else seemed to be up, except the servants and the children.

Several doors away and one floor down, Lord William stirred in his sleep. Had he heard Caroline's voice? Or had he heard Miss Snow? Perhaps something had happened and he ought to get up. Alas, his thoughts of the enchanting governess had kept him awake until after midnight and he craved sleep.

He buried his face in the pillow. But he was doomed. Charlie pounded on his door and entered.

"Kittens! Uncle, get up! Nefret had kittens! Four kittens!"

"Congratulate her for me. I want to sleep. Go away."

"Miss Snow and Caro are already downstairs," the boy said eagerly. "They did not even bother to change out of their nightclothes. You must get up!"

Lord William cracked one eye open. This was interesting news, insofar as it concerned Miss Snow.

"Very well, Charlie. If you insist, I will visit the new mother—where did you say she had the kittens?"

"I didn't say! In the kitchen!" the boy called, racing out the door again.

Lord William sat up groggily and swung his legs over the side of the bed. There were his breeches, and there, his linen shirt. He pulled on enough clothing to look respectable, threw a silk robe over it, and gave up on finding his slippers.

Not a minute later he was in the kitchen. Caroline knelt by a basket filled with what seemed to be a heap of multicolored fur but was really a mother cat and four newborn kittens, under the watchful eye of Mrs. Diggory.

Lord William scarcely knew what to say. Miss Snow stood to one side, smiling radiantly, looking more beautiful than his sweetest dreams of her. Her honey-colored hair tumbled over her shoulders and her face was still rosy with sleep. The lace edge of her pillowcase had left a small mark upon one cheek, which he longed to touch. He could well imagine her lovely face upon a pillow next to his—

"Look at the kittens, Uncle William," Caroline said in a soft voice. "They are so soft and so tiny. Nefret let me pet one but Miss Snow said I mustn't pick them up."

"She will hide them if she thinks they will be bothered," the housekeeper said. "They might not be safe somewhere else."

"Can they see?" Charles said.

"Not yet," Mrs. Diggory answered. "Their eyes will not open for a few weeks more."

"Can we make them little clothes, Miss Snow?" Caroline asked.

Emma laughed. "They have no need of clothes, Caro, or anything else. Their mama will keep them warm and fed."

"Nefret knows just what to do," Mrs. Diggory added. She looked up at the sound of the kitchen door opening. Jamie entered.

"Ah, the great day has come." He crossed the kitchen and knelt by Caroline to peer into the basket. "Four wee kittens! Just look at that!"

"Shh," Caroline whispered. "Mrs. Diggory said we should be quiet."

"Aye, little lass." He got up a little stiffly. "Och. My knees do ache. I expect it will rain today."

Charlie, who now sat on the floor beside his sister, looked curiously at Jamie. "Do knees foretell the weather?"

"Aye."

"But the sky is clear," Charlie said.

"Not fer long. It will rain, I'm tellin' ye."

"Do you have knees like that, Uncle?" the boy asked.

Lord William laughed. "Not yet."

Jamie cast an approving eye upon the housekeeper's buxom form. "How is it that you are dressed, Mary Diggory, when everyone else is in their nightclothes?"

"I never undressed, Mr. Crichton."

Bertha entered the kitchen from her small room off the pantry, rubbing her eyes. "What she means is that she stayed with that there cat until them kittens came. Mrs. Diggory gets her tay first. Now get out, all of ye."

Lord William cast her an indignant look. "Am I to be ordered about by a cook?"

"Aye," Jamie said cheerfully. "Ye are a laird, but a cook is th' ruler of her kitchen."

"I see."

"Beggin' yer pardon, sir," Bertha said. "I can't work with so many about."

There was no arguing with her. Excepting the servants, they went back to their respective bed-chambers, dressed themselves properly, and came down to their breakfast later.

Lady Barbara, whom no one had thought to summon, slept on, for which Emma was grateful. They had the breakfast room to themselves and they seemed so much like a family—just her and Lord William and the children—that Emma wanted the feeling of closeness never to end. The long-awaited arrival of the kittens had put everyone in a happy mood. Even Caroline, who was often cross upon awakening, seemed sunny as the day itself.

Lord William, just returned from his morning ride, had brought in the post. Emma felt a faint stirring of unease.

Perhaps there would be a communication from the Kents, announcing their return from Egypt or a letter from Mrs. Bumpus proclaiming a miraculous cure in the odorous waters of Bath. But there seemed to be nothing of importance today. Lord William opened envelopes with his butter knife and glanced only briefly at the letters within.

Caroline talked of nothing but the kittens, deciding upon various names but changing her mind every five minutes.

"Call them Fee, Fie, Fo, and Fum," Charlie said impatiently.

"I will get them mixed up if I do."

"Caroline, just write down the names you like in your book," Emma said. "The matter does not need to be decided today."

"But does Nefret know which is which?" the little girl said anxiously.

"Of course, dear," Emma said. "Mothers always know."

"I will write to Mama today," Caroline said plaintively. "And I shall tell her all about the kittens."

With a guilty start, Emma realized how long it had been since she had posted a letter to the vicarage. "That is an excellent idea, Caroline. We shall both write to our mothers. I miss mine as well. Your mama will be delighted to hear from you and I shall help you with your penmanship and spelling."

"Thank you, Miss Snow."

"What about me?" Charlie asked. "I would rather be outdoors. I don't believe Jamie. It won't rain."

Lord William smiled. "Look for Robbie at the stable. He told me that he saw an otter near the brook."

"An otter! May I go, Miss Snow?"

"Yes, of course. I don't mind."

Lord William turned his attention to his niece. "Caroline, perhaps you can persuade your dear mama to bring at least one of the kittens home with you when you leave Cranley Hall."

Caroline narrowed her eyes. "Only one?"

"Well, I think Mrs. Diggory wants a cat, Caroline. And Jamie asked if he might have one."

"And I will bring one to my parents when I leave," Emma said suddenly. "That way, Caroline, you will know where Nefret's children are and you can even visit them."

She looked around at three stricken faces. Oh, dear. Perhaps she should not take a kitten after all.

"But you are not leaving us just yet, Miss Snow," Lord William began.

Caroline burst into tears. "No! You cannot go! Mrs. Bumpus will come back from Bath—Charlie said she would!"

"Not quite, Caro," the boy said, not wanting to repeat the rest of his conversation with his sister, especially not the part about his uncle possibly being in love with Miss Snow.

"Caroline, I have no plans to leave at the moment. Please calm yourself."

The little girl shut her writing book and took a deep breath. "Am I being a silly goose? Charlie says I am sometimes." Caroline took another deep breath that turned into a sniffing sort of honk. "I sound like one!" She giggled and her brother grinned.

"You do, Caro."

There. The awkwardness between the four of them dissolved in an instant. Emma studied Lord William's handsome profile as he returned to the task of opening letters. He no longer seemed sad, but finding that the thought of her departure affected him so strongly was encouraging.

She was right. She *had* seen the look of love in his eyes.

* * *

The rain that Jamie Crichton's knees had predicted in the morning began later that afternoon as heavy clouds covered the sky.

A steady drizzle turned into a downpour and from that, into a deluge. Water coursed through the fresh earth of the garden, cutting channels between the new plants and exposing the roots of many.

Lord William looked down at the wreckage from the library window. He had locked the door, giving in to a blue-deviled mood that he could not shake. It was not just the sudden storm that made the air so heavy and time seem to stop.

No, it was Miss Snow's innocent mention of writing to her mama and, worse, of returning to her own home. Certainly her family must love her dearly and she would naturally want to be with them, far away, and not here with him.

Damn it all. She could not leave Cranley Hall. He had grown accustomed to her delightful presence. Perhaps he ought not to wait as he had planned.

What if she were to meet another man? And what if that man were richer, taller, titled, and the owner of a house that was not in perpetual danger of collapsing? Lord William wondered if the best man—meaning himself, of course—would still win Emma's heart.

His fine dreams of proposing to her in a year's time, when the garden was abloom, were just that—dreams.

The damned garden was well on its way to the river, thanks to the pounding rain. Would she ever see it in bloom if she left? He had given little thought to that awful day.

How could he keep Emma—dear, darling, doe-eyed Emma—from walking out of his life? He had nothing to offer her but Cranley Hall, crumbling away in the grand manner, and a kitten.

True, she was a vicar's daughter, with no pedigree or fortune, but he loved her passionately, self-restraint be damned. He had never felt anything quite so intense. If only Edward were here, he might ask him for advice—well, no. His scholarly, shy brother was not the sort of person who had ever experienced passion.

But Edward did seem quite happy with Elizabeth, so his brother must know something. Precisely what that might be, Lord William was not sure. Edward and Elizabeth shared a love of learning, a love of adventure, and seemed to adore their children, if from a great distance at times.

Curious.

What did he and Emma have in common? A borrowed niece and nephew, a mutual dislike of peacocks, and a mania for reading. Oh, and they had shared three splendid kisses under a sky filled with exploding stars. Was that enough for a life-long union of souls?

Lord William decided that it might be. He could imagine no other woman than Emma at his side.

He went back to his desk and the paperwork he had begun, determined to ignore the rain and his melancholy mood.

* * *

Emma and Caroline had moved to the drawing room to begin the day's lessons. The letters to their respective mamas had been written, blotted, and put into envelopes to be sent tomorrow.

No one would be going into town to post them today. The driving rain beat steadily against the windowpanes. Emma busied herself with small tasks, trimming a new quill and refilling the inkbottle so that Caroline might practice her penmanship a little longer or draw.

Charlie had gone out while the sun was still shining to talk to Robbie about the otter.

He had promised not to bring it home. He had also promised to return by afternoon.

Emma wondered where he was. It was not quite time to worry, but considering Charles's penchant for getting into scrapes, perhaps she ought to start. Still, the boy knew his way about the countryside for miles around and if he got wet and muddy, it would do him no lasting harm.

His uncle did not seem to mind.

She watched Caroline set pen to paper. Uneven rows of *p*'s and *q*'s appeared, but the little girl soon grew bored with making letters. She turned a very large *p* into a pointy-eared cat, giving it long whiskers with calligraphic flourishes.

"Very good, Caroline! You have a wonderful imagination."

"Thank you, Miss Snow. I shall make kittens for my cat."

Concentrating hard and sticking out the tip of her small tongue, Caroline added a row of kittens with even longer whiskers.

A thundering sound filled the room before

Emma realized that it was not thunder at all but someone charging up the stairs. Robbie, soaked through, burst into the room and stood dripping on the carpet.

"Whatever is the matter?" Emma asked.

"Ch-Charlie—took a boat. He is out upon the river, miss."

"What? Charlie can swim but he does not know how to row—and what on earth were you two doing in the boathouse? It is on someone else's land and it is nearly a mile away!"

"That is where I saw the otter, miss."

"I did not think to ask him where he was going," said Emma, feeling a flash of guilt. "Oh, what shall we do?"

"Uncle will know," Caroline said.

"Yes, of course. Robbie, run to the library and tell Lord William what has happened! Go!"

Caroline set down her pen and looked at Emma with wide, frightened eyes. "What will happen to Charlie?"

"He will be all right, Caroline. But we must find him. Go down to the kitchen and visit the kittens. Nefret will be glad to see you."

"Yes, Miss Snow." She left the room with a worried look upon her face that nearly broke Emma's heart.

Lord William entered the drawing room seconds later.

"Did Robbie tell you what happened, my lord? Should we go to the boathouse?"

"No. Charlie must have floated downriver. I will take a horse and ride on to the bridge. You must stay here, Miss Snow." He turned to leave as quickly as he had come.

"Yes, sir. I mean, no, I will come with you!" She ran out to the hall and watched Lord William take the stairs two at a time.

"You will be more hindrance than help!" he called.

"But I must . . ." Her voice died away. If Caroline was safe in the kitchen with Mrs. Diggory or Bertha—Emma would peek in to make sure—she would join the search, no matter what Lord William said.

The brook went to the river, she knew that much. Emma followed it, taking care not to slip on the muddy banks. Her dress and shoes were drenched but she did not care. The late summer rain was curiously warm and her exertions made her warmer still.

She saw the blurry outlines of a small building—was it the boathouse? She had never come this far. It looked like a boathouse. She pushed her wet hair away from her face and took a shortcut across a field.

She tried the back door. It was unlocked. Emma stepped inside. The rain drummed on the roof overhead, leaking down in a few places. The inside of the boathouse had the greenish, ghostly look of a place that had not been entered for some time.

Even on this dismal day, reflections of the river outside the open door to the dock played upon the walls, as if they were made of water and not wood.

She saw a freshly scraped line on the slimy floor where a boat had been dragged out to the dock. Another rowboat leaned against the wall, but it had a jagged hole in its side, made long ago by the looks of it.

Emma ran out onto the dock. "Charlie! Charlie, where are you?"

There was no answer. Swollen by the heavy rain, the river was moving swiftly—much more swiftly than when she had been out on it with Lord William. Huge, leafy branches, tangled with debris, floated by. Her heart sank. Even if she could take the other rowboat and look for him, what good would it do? The men would have to rescue her and Charlie, and this was no time for foolhardy heroics.

It was just as well that the other boat had a hole in its side. She decided to continue on foot. The strong current might sweep away a small rowboat—or ram it into the rocks nearer the bank.

Emma prayed that Charlie was safe.

She left the boathouse and went on, pushing wind-whipped branches out of her way. Her progress was difficult and how far she had come, Emma did not know. She kept close to the banks but not so close she was in danger herself, heeding Lord William's warning that she would prove more hindrance than help. She called for Charlie, again and again.

A cry floated back upon the wind. "Here! Over here!"

Emma peered through the rain, trying to see. She ran on. There he was, close to shore as she had hoped but—dear heavens! The rowboat was half-filled with water and caught upon a rock. Charlie clung to its sides, panicked.

She reached him in no time. "Throw me the rope!"

He would not let go.

"Charlie!" she shrieked. "Help is coming!" If she had to go out and get him, by God, she would. But she would surely drown without the rope—if only he would let go and throw it! She would tie it to a tree and wade out—but was the rope long enough to reach from the boat to the shore?

She turned at the sudden thunder of hooves behind her, and the sound of Lord William's voice. "Damnation! I told you to stay home!"

He dismounted swiftly, every bit as wet as she was, and took a coil of rope from his saddle, tossing one end to the Cranley Hall groom who followed him on another horse, jumping down in the blink of an eye.

"Tie it?" the groom asked.

"Yes! Make it fast to that tree and hang on for dear life, man," he muttered. "Charlie, I am coming!"

He looped the other end around his waist, knotted it securely and waded out in the river.

"Uncle! We will both drown!"

"Be still, Charlie! And do not tip the damned boat!"

The foaming water was only up to Lord William's waist but the current was still swift and strong. Emma watched him nervously as he went further. Little by little he went on, slipping only once just before he gained the rowboat. He cursed. Standing up again was a struggle but he managed it.

"Come to me."

Charlie's grip relaxed. He reached out to his uncle, but slipped inside the boat, flailing his arms wildly.

"Try again! You must stay calm, boy!"

Charlie reached for him once more, clasping Lord William's strong arms. He gasped with relief and let his uncle lift him up and over the gunwales. Lord William put him over one broad shoulder and steadied him with a hand.

"Back to terra firma, Charlie. Tighten the rope," he called to the groom, "but do not pull me over!"

He walked slowly but surely, aided by the taut rope, with his nephew upon his shoulder as if the boy weighed nothing at all.

Emma just stood there, stunned into silence. The rain had eased but the current had not, and Lord William could scarcely stay on his feet.

She watched him stagger onto the bank at last, reaching a hand out to the waiting groom who pulled man and boy the last few steps to safety.

"There is a blanket in my saddlebag. Put it around him, Johnny."

The groom found it, and wrapped Charlie in it.

The boy was shivering. "I am s-sorry—so s-sorry. Will there be c-consequences, Uncle?"

"I think you have learned your lesson," Lord William answered quietly. "No. I will not punish you. It was I who told you about the otter."

"But I took the b-boat—Robbie told me not t-to but I did not listen. The storm c-came on so qu-quickly—"

"Hush. We must return to Cranley Hall. I have no blanket for Miss Snow."

He strode over to where she was standing and she trembled. What would he say? She felt suddenly numb.

"It is a good thing that the other boat had a hole in one side, or you might have taken it, Miss Snow. Am I right?"

"How did you know about the hole?"

"I put it there when I was a lad. On just such an adventure." He looked down at Charlie and returned his gaze to Emma. "You are brave, Miss Snow. If you had not gone along the bank and called so loudly, we might not have found him in time. He has you to thank."

She gulped. "No."

He smiled slightly. "An eloquent reply. It will have to do. Help her up, Johnny. She will ride with me, and Charlie can ride with you."

He swung up into his saddle, and waited for her. The groom lifted her up and Emma—drenched, muddy, frightened Emma—settled back against Lord William's chest.

CHAPTER 10

Emma came down with the worst cold of her life the very next day. Mrs. Diggory bundled her in blankets, made up chest plasters that stung, and brewed alarming concoctions to clear her poor patient's head. Emma drank them dutifully. At least she could not taste them.

Her woes multiplied. A racking cough made her tired and her ears buzzed. She was miserable.

A week of confinement to her bedchamber went by in a blur. She rather liked being waited on hand and foot, and that was her sole consolation. Bertha prepared special beef broth and sent it up on a tray with toast. Emma sipped and nibbled, and went back to sleep.

She was relieved that Susie Trelawny had come from the inn to look after the children while she was ill. Mrs. Diggory said that Susie was a dab hand in the kitchen and good company. She added rather slyly that Winkworth seemed smitten with the girl.

When Emma could sit up without coughing, she

saw through the window that the great storm had left the surrounding countryside somewhat the worse for wear. The crops in the field were flattened and many trees had lost branches, down to the great old oaks.

Soon enough, it would recover, just like her. Jamie had set about repairing the damage to the Cranley Hall garden and neat rows of plants appeared once more.

At last Emma was deemed well enough to move to the drawing room during the day. Mrs. Diggory still insisted on swaddling Emma in knitted shawls and itchy scarves, which she mostly removed when the housekeeper left the room.

Caroline brought her writing things and her schoolbooks into the drawing room, and was good as gold when it came to amusing herself, so as not to trouble her governess.

Emma was touched. Charlie, convinced that his rash act had caused her to catch cold—well, perhaps it had—would appear at odd moments with bouquets of summer wildflowers and inquire in a manly way as to her welfare.

Lord William kept a more watchful eye on the boy these days, making sure that Charlie had plenty of work to do and that it was done.

He had come in to see her several times. His visits cheered her more than anything, but Emma did wish that she did not look so pale and that the circles under her eyes would go away.

Whenever she heard him knock, she rubbed her cheeks to bring a bit of color into them and sat up straighter. Being an invalid was a wretched experience, in her opinion, and she was determined not to look like one.

Emma was alone at the moment, since Caroline had gone to the kitchen to visit the kittens and sit with Mrs. Diggory and Susan. She leaned back in the armchair, thinking again of how delicious it had been to lean against Lord William's chest during their journey through the weakening storm.

That alone had been worth catching cold for.

His undeniable strength and the warmth of his big body had instantly taken away her fear at seeing Charlie in such peril. The wild ride home had thrilled her to her core. Lord William clasped the reins in one hand and held her close with the other, but with a gentle ease, as if he rescued damsels in distress all the time.

If only being a damsel in distress was something one could do again and again!

Once they had pulled up in front of Cranley Hall, a footman had helped her and Charles alight and brought them inside to Mrs. Diggory straightaway. The capable housekeeper had taken over from there.

Charles had suffered no ill effects, unlike Emma. Though forced to stay in bed for a day or two, his bright eyes and high spirits were enough to convince everyone that the boy was quite well. His uncle had allowed him to go about as usual.

She wondered what Lord William was doing and where he was. She had heard whispering in the hall not too long ago, but the buzzing in her ears had not entirely gone away. She could not make out who was whispering, or why.

Decidedly masculine footsteps came closer . . . and stopped outside the drawing room door. There—that was his knock. She bit her lips, pinched her cheeks, and patted her hair in the few seconds it took for the doorknob to turn.

Caroline entered first, followed by Lord William, carrying a very fine doll's house.

"Look what we found, Miss Snow!"

Emma looked first at Lord William, who was beaming in an avuncular way, and then at the doll's house he held. It was a perfect replica of Cranley Hall, every detail reproduced to scale.

"It was in the attic in a locked closet. Caro wanted to know what was behind that door and made me fetch the key. The children have a secret lair up there, you know."

"Have you, Caroline? What else is hidden there?"

"Oh, a missing cushion or two. And scattered toys to trip over."

"I forgot to pick them up," Caroline protested. "But I will."

"Very good. See that you do. Now shall we let Miss Snow look at Cranley Hall as it used to be?"

Caroline cleared her things from the low table by Emma and Lord William set the house down with great care. "Uncle says that his great-grand-papa had it made when this house was built."

"It is a wonderful thing," Emma said, peering into its glass-paned windows. "Look, it has furniture in every room. And a chandelier!"

Lord William laughed. "I thought you would enjoy it. I had quite forgotten its existence, though I did see it once or twice when I was a child. I suppose it was taken up to the attic for safekeeping."

Caroline sat down on the carpet and spread her skirts about her. "Shall we play with it, Miss Snow? I believe it is educational."

"Not in the least. But it will be great fun, Caroline."

Lord William watched the two of them take out miniature pieces of furniture and exclaim over each one, testing the tiny hinges on the cabinets and admiring the workmanship.

"I will leave you to it. If you need anything, Caro, ask Mrs. Diggory. We do not want Miss Snow to exert herself until she is entirely well."

He lingered for a few more moments, quite unwilling to leave, if truth be told. The sight of Emma and Caroline, the imaginary mistresses of a very small Cranley Hall, was an endearing one.

"Thank you so much, Uncle." Caroline got up to give him a kiss and twined her arms about his neck, rumpling his carefully tied cloth and making him smile.

"You are most welcome, my dear."

He gave Emma a tender look that made her blush. Whatever was he thinking? She murmured a word or two of polite farewell as he left the room, and turned again to the doll's house.

"When the kittens are bigger, they can play in it, Miss Snow," Caroline said, settling down again. "They are growing fast. I wanted to bring them to you in a basket, but Mrs. Diggory says I must not disturb them."

"Quite right," Emma nodded. "They will be scampering all over the house soon enough, I expect."

Caroline put a hand into the kitchen of the miniature Cranley Hall and turned the spit upon the hearth. "Look! It works! But our kitchen has different pots and pans—and a different table."

"Of course. Houses never stay the same for long."

"Yes, Miss Snow. Did Uncle tell you that the storm

broke things? He needs money to fix our roof and must go to London soon," Caroline said.

Emma felt a pang. Lord William had not breathed a word of the damage, no doubt because she had been so ill. "No, Caroline. I am sorry to hear that."

Dear old Cranley Hall. She felt more and more at home here. Its very shabbiness seemed welcoming to her, though its former grandeur was still evident.

Over the course of the summer, she had entered nearly every room, and found out most of the house's secrets and forgotten places. The ivy-covered ballroom that stood apart from the house was the only place she had not seen.

"He says Mrs. Bumpus is coming back," Caroline added. "He had a letter from her yesterday."

Oh, dear. So that was that. With the children's real governess around, there would be no need for Emma to stay.

What if Mrs. Bumpus arrived while Lord William was gone? She might. His journey from Devon to London and back again would take many days. Emma would have to be very polite so as not to hurt her feelings. The old lady had pride of place, after all.

Emma hated the idea of being in the way, rather like Lady Barbara, who *still* had not left Cranley Hall. Barbara, a stickler for form if not feeling, had conveyed her concern for Miss Snow in a brief note, obviously afraid that she might catch Emma's cold.

Mrs. Diggory had delivered it to Emma with a sniff, remarking that her ladyship was getting too comfortable for her own good.

"Shall I fetch my dolls, Miss Snow? I think they would like the house," Caroline said.

"Yes, dear. But I might nap." Emma felt suddenly weary. "And then we can read together."

Caroline nodded. "I shall be very, very quiet. Mrs. Diggory said I must be good so you can get well. We all want you to get well, Miss Snow."

She picked up the knitted shawls and scarf that Emma had set aside and piled them upon her governess's lap. "Mrs. Diggory says you should not take these warm things off. She knows that you do, Miss Snow."

"And how does she know that, Caroline?"

The little girl smiled pertly. "I told her."

"Imp!"

Caroline scampered away and Emma looked after her fondly. Everyone at Cranley Hall had proved to be a true friend. Leaving was quite unthinkable. Therefore, she decided not to think about it for one more second.

Upstairs in his library, Lord William returned to the household accounts. The money to fix the roof would have to come from somewhere, but he could not squeeze another penny out of what he had.

The numbers seemed to swim upon the page. He slammed the ledger shut. There was nothing for it. He would have to go to London and talk to his friend, Gerald Mixton, who seemed to be able to make money out of thin air.

At least Mixton's advice had always proved sound. Unfortunately, on the general principle of not putting all his eggs in one basket, Lord William had listened to other financial wizards from time to time, and lost his shirt when he did.

How did Mixton do it? His friend seemed to

learn everything he needed to know by haunting London coffee-houses, where he heard first of investments that he could buy cheap and sell dear.

Never touch your capital. That was one of Gerald Mixton's favorite mottoes. *Live below your means.* That was another.

Mixton did not gamble, kept an inexpensive mistress, and dressed in sober clothes that had never been in fashion and therefore would never go out.

Lord William had lived just as modestly, and yet he was poor, relatively speaking. The significant difference between him and his friend was that Mixton Grange had been perfectly preserved by generations of industrious Mixtons.

Gerald did not pay interest upon ruinous mortgages, and his tenants' carefully managed farms returned thousands in rents. He thought it best to knock down Cranley Hall and start over.

But Lord William could not bring himself to do that. Though he would not, most likely, inherit the house or its lands, his two older brothers had no interest whatsoever in any of it.

William wanted to be here and make a go of the estate by any means possible.

He was nearly thirty. It was time to settle down. He had done what was expected of young gentlemen, poked through ruins in Greece and Rome, and looked at dusty paintings in Italian churches on the grand tour, and lived in London. But the green hills of Devon were the only place on earth that seemed like home to him.

Especially with Miss Emma Snow in residence at Cranley Hall.

His admiration for her grew stronger day by day.

Her feminine charm bewitched him and her spirited intelligence was a force to be reckoned with. And now he knew that she possessed uncommon courage as well. No simpering miss would have run out into the rain to rescue Charlie as she had.

He had felt rather like a knight—in sopping clothes and not shining armor, to be sure—when they had ridden home on that dark day. The sensation of her sweet body so close to his in that thin, wet dress had driven him nearly mad. No wonder he had slept so poorly since.

Damn, damn, damn. He put his head in his hands. Dearest Emma. She could not stay much longer and he had no idea how to tell her that. He picked up the letter that had come from Mrs. Bumpus and tore it in half.

No decent man would keep *two* governesses under his roof. It didn't matter that the Dreadful Bumpus was unattractive and older than his mother. People would talk. Miss Snow's reputation would be ruined forever, and her parents would never forgive him, to say nothing of Edward and Elizabeth. He could not face the righteous wrath of that many people.

How could he explain any of that to Emma?

If Miss Snow stayed here, he could not court her in the eminently respectable way he had planned: from the safe distance of Mixton Grange, with the approval of her parents, and so on. Though he now felt it would be the height of foolishness to take a year to pop the question, he still wanted to do the right thing.

Perhaps the solution was to marry Emma at once. He picked up his quill to pen a letter to her that would clearly express his predicament and his feelings. Before he dipped the quill into the ink, he thought better of it.

You have not a feather to fly with.

He threw the quill across the room.

CHAPTER 11

A few weeks later . . .

Emma was still not completely well, though she had consumed gallons of Mrs. Diggory's medicinal teas and equal quantities of Bertha's best broth. She wrapped herself up to her ears in shawls and blankets, and tried to look healthy. No one was convinced. Her mother had been sent for.

She sank down into the drawing room sofa. Autumn had come and the house was decidedly colder. Mrs. Diggory made sure that the maid kept a fire going in whatever room Emma was in.

She looked down at her lap. She could not move in any case. Nefret would have something to say about it. At Caroline's insistence, the kittens had been brought in an hour ago.

Emma had not seen them for a while. Though they still slept much of the time, they were enchanting balls of fluff when they were awake, meowing and climbing all over each other on shaky little legs, and even emitting tiny hisses.

Their eyes had recently opened and were a startling blue but they still could not see very well. Their markings were much clearer now. Three were striped, like Blimey, and one was the color of desert sand, like Nefret.

Caroline had taken them out of the basket one by one and put them into Emma's lap, watched nervously by Nefret.

The Egyptian cat jumped up and curled around her kittens. They had settled down and now all of them were purring, four high, one low, in feline harmony. The sound was soothing. Caroline stayed nearby and redecorated her dollhouse as Charlie read a book of natural history.

"Miss Snow, did you know that polar bears are not at all playful?"

Emma smiled. "I am not surprised. They are very large animals and they are carnivores."

"But still . . . they look playful."

"Are you planning to acquire one?"

"No. Well, someday perhaps." He returned to his book.

Susie Trelawny entered with a tray of small sandwiches and biscuits with jam inside. "Hallo, Miss Snow. How're ye keeping?"

"Well enough, Susie. Thank you."

"Mrs. Diggory thought the children might want summat to eat."

They gathered round and took a plate each, which they quickly filled. Caroline heaped hers with biscuits. She split one in half and began to lick off the jam.

"Now, now. That's not nice, Caro," Susie said sternly.

"But I only like the jam!"

Susie shook her head. "What about you, Miss Snow?"

"I promise you that I will never lick jam off a biscuit, Susie." Emma extended a hand from underneath her woolly cocoon and took half a sandwich. The kittens stirred and their mother gazed up at Susie with huge golden eyes.

"Just look at that cat!" Susie laughed. "She seems quite comfy. I wasn't sure if Caroline should bring the kittens here, but Mrs. D. said it was all right."

Emma stroked Nefret's head. "They are pleasant company." She took a bite of her sandwich.

"Have more. You must eat, even if you don't feel like it. Have a biscuit. Have two biscuits."

Emma laughed. "You sound exactly like my mother."

"She will soon be here, Miss Snow. We have prepared the bedroom next to Lady Barbara for her. But she probably will not stay longer than one night. I expect your mother will want to take you home straightaway."

Caroline turned around in a flash, putting on her most tragic expression. "Miss Snow can't go."

"Emma's mother will decide and not you, little miss."

Caroline pouted. "The Dreadful Bumpus is coming. Uncle said so. He wishes he had a portcullis."

"Now what is that?" Susie asked. "And who is the Dreadful Bumpus?"

"A portcullis is the big iron gate of a castle,"

Charlie explained. "You drop it on your enemies to keep them from getting in. Mrs. Bumpus used to be our governess, before Emma."

Susie picked up the tray. "Is she your enemy, then?"

"Certainly not." Lord William's deep voice made them all sit up straight. He walked into the room without knocking. "Caro, you must not repeat everything you hear. Children, we have a visitor."

Charles and Caroline got up and brushed the crumbs from their clothes. "Very good. I expect you to behave in a civilized fashion, however strange it may seem. I fear that letting you run wild this summer was a mistake."

"Am I civilized now?" Caroline asked worriedly.

"More or less. Except for the jam around your mouth. But our visitor might not care. She is a mother."

"My mother?" Emma sat up with difficulty, considering that her lap was full of kittens and a sleepy cat.

"Yes."

She heard the front door open and close, and the sound of a fluty, warbling voice that was utterly familiar and extraordinarily comforting.

"Mama! Oh, someone tell her I cannot get up— no, don't tell her that! She will think I am gravely ill!"

Lord William nodded. "As you wish. Winkworth will bring her in. Caro, put the kittens in the basket and take them back to the kitchen."

"Yes, Uncle." Caroline collected them quickly, assisted by Susie, who had set down the tray, and Charlie. The three left the room together.

Emma rose from her chair and smoothed her dress. She dashed over to the mirror. Oh, dear. She was dreadfully pale and her hair looked a fright.

"You look unwell," he said tenderly.

"What?" She turned to see Lord William studying her.

"You need your mother's care, Miss Snow. I wish you did not have to go."

"Who told you I was going, sir?"

"It doesn't matter."

"Hush!" Emma put a finger to her lips. Light footsteps approached, followed by the measured tread of a man. No doubt her mother had gone ahead, not being the sort of person who stood on ceremony or waited for directions.

Lord William looked only mildly alarmed.

"We should not be in a room with a closed door, either." Emma opened it cautiously—and there was her mama. Winkworth, a few steps behind the old lady, nodded to Lord William.

Mrs. Snow reached out to embrace her daughter with a joyful cry and a few tears. Lord William watched the happy reunion with a smile on his face.

Letting go of Emma at last and wiping her eyes, Mrs. Snow came into the drawing room. "Ooh, this is a splendid room . . . in its way." Her gaze swept over the furniture, missing nothing.

He was not sure what the old lady meant—mayhap the velvet armchair, which was still missing a cushion. Was she sizing up the house and him? Perhaps she had expected more.

Why on earth did he feel so deucedly awkward? Mrs. Snow was not of his rank—but damn it all, she *was* Emma's mother. What did rank matter? He bowed. "Welcome to Cranley Hall, Mrs. Snow."

"Thank you, my lord. I am very glad to be here and to see my dear daughter."

"Of course."

"Where are the children, Emma? And the cats? I should like to explore this great house and meet everyone in it. You only wrote one letter, my dear, and I am so curious!"

Emma blushed at her mother's forwardness. "My apologies, Mama. Cranley Hall is indeed a fascinating place. The housekeeper has prepared a bedroom just for you and you may stay as long as you like."

"My own bedroom! No snoring husband! Ooh, I shall be very happy. Thank you, my dear. And thank you, Lord William."

Lord William merely nodded. Emma's impulsive offer might prove disastrous. *As long as you like* was a slippery slope, in his experience. He had expected that the old lady would stay a day or two, then take her daughter home to recover fully. He could then set his plan in motion.

Of course, he did not mind a brief visit since the old lady had traveled so far, but her shrewd and instantaneous appraisal of his beloved house had unnerved him. He got the distinct feeling that Mrs. Snow was not impressed. What if she thought he was not good enough for her daughter?

All his plans and schemes would be for naught.

When Mrs. Snow walked to the window to look out upon the grounds, he took Emma aside and whispered, "Are you not returning home with your dear mama? What of your health?"

He gazed deeply into her eyes, willing her to understand his reasons for wanting her to leave. *If you do, I can begin to court you at once without compromising your reputation or my own. I would rather not be spoken of as the wicked seducer of an innocent governess. It is so hard to live that sort of thing down, you know. Please understand, darling Emma.*

She gazed back, looking mesmerized, but she seemed unable to read his mind. He would have to explain. But not here and not now. Mrs. Snow turned from the window and cast another appraising glance at the drawing room, not seeming to see how close he was to Emma. He moved sideways with one great step, as if participating in a parlor game.

The sun streaming in showed the worn spots on the upholstery, he realized with chagrin. He moved to stand directly upon the hole in the carpet.

"Well, well. I would love a nice cup of tea," Mrs. Snow chirped.

Lord William nodded. "An excellent idea." He went out into the hall to find Winkworth.

Emma whispered in her mother's ear. "Whatever happens, Mama, please do not insist on taking me home."

"I had not thought about it one way or another, Emma dear. I only came to take care of you. But why do you not want to leave?"

"I will tell you later when we are alone."

"As you wish."

She smiled brightly at Lord William when he returned a few seconds later and announced that tea would be served and the children sent in. He excused himself from partaking, however.

* * *

When the hour grew late, Mrs. Snow was weary. She had met everyone in the household, including Caroline and Charlie.

They wanted to know all about their new governess's childhood. Had Emma ever been naughty and if so, how? Did she practice her penmanship? Had she really memorized the encyclopedia by the age of four, as she had told them? Mrs. Snow answered patiently enough but she was unused to such inquisitiveness from children. She could not remember Emma asking so many questions.

The old lady was glad indeed when Susie Trelawny came in to take the Kent children upstairs to bed. She turned to Emma.

"No wonder you are exhausted, my dear. Are they always like that?"

"No. But they are bright and curious."

"Still, you will never get well if they will not leave you alone."

"I don't mind, Mama. I have grown very fond of them."

Mrs. Snow was silent for a moment. "Tell me, Emma dear, if I am mistaken, but are you not fond of their uncle as well?"

"Perhaps."

"I thought so. Is that why you wish to stay?"

Emma twisted the handkerchief in her hands almost into rope. "If I come home to you and Papa, Lord William will forget all about me."

Mrs. Snow looked at her shrewdly. "I doubt that very much." Despite her recent illness, Emma was lovelier than ever. Lord William was quite obviously enamored of her. Mrs. Snow had known it the moment she had walked into the drawing room.

It was all in the way he looked at her daughter—and how nervous he seemed to meet her mama, very much on his best behavior and not lordly in the least. Mrs. Snow smiled to herself.

"So much has changed in such a short time, Mama. Cranley Hall seems like home to me now. I am very happy here. And I cannot leave Caroline and Charles until Mrs. Bumpus comes back."

"Ah, yes. Their first governess. Your father mentioned her name but I know nothing about her." The woman could well be her daughter's rival for the attentions of Lord William. Mrs. Snow imagined her in the most unflattering terms. *A scrawny widow-woman with a hungry look in her eyes. No better than she should be. Hoping to marry above her station.*

Though this last was precisely what Mrs. Snow wanted for Emma, she thought nothing of putting social climbing on Mrs. Bumpus's list of sins.

"I have not met her but I know she is a dreadful old dragon," Emma blurted out. "The children do not like her and neither does Lord William."

Mrs. Snow brightened. "Well, then. You have every chance of marrying him yourself."

"Mama! What are you saying?"

"You heard me."

"I—I have feelings for him. And I think that he has feelings for me. But he has not declared himself."

"Has he trifled with you?"

"No!"

Suspicious of so vehement a denial, Mrs. Snow looked closely at her daughter. "What has he done?"

"Oh, Mama." Emma twisted her handkerchief a little more. "He kissed me."

"Where? When?"

"On the lips. During the fireworks at the Berryfield Fair."

Her mother looked faintly shocked. "Lips? Has it gone that far?"

"Yes. I mean—no. Oh, Mama! I don't know what to do!"

Mrs. Snow permitted herself a smile. "Hm. One must make a man believe that he will get everything he wants and then not give it. Of course, you might try ignoring him if that does not work."

"Surely that was not how—you did not use such tricks on Papa, did you? Oh—oh, never mind."

"Your papa was not always so proper, Emma. He had a bit of dash once."

Could it be true? Was her dear, stodgy, utterly predictable Papa ever dashing? Yet Emma supposed he would not have been attracted to her lively mother otherwise. Life was strange. Love was even stranger.

"Mama, my head aches. Let us go to bed. We can talk more tomorrow."

"Of course, my dear. Lead the way."

Emma assisted her mother from her chair and they left the room arm in arm.

CHAPTER 12

Two more weeks later . . .

Lord William's plan had been well and truly scotched. Now that Emma's mama was here, everything had changed.

He paced the front hall, not sure whether to go out for a walk or have Winkworth bring up a bottle of sherry to the library so he could drink it and sulk.

Emma was ignoring him. It was most upsetting. It had gone on too long.

Her mother had announced right away that her daughter was far too delicate to travel. Mrs. Snow then took over the kitchen, much to Bertha's indignation. There she produced vats of custard—bland, slippery stuff that Emma adored. It did seem to have a strengthening effect, though Mrs. Snow still did not consider her daughter fully recovered.

But Emma looked quite healthy to Lord William.

However, he was only a man, as Mrs. Snow often said, and what did he know?

Perhaps he ought to eat quantities of custard. It might give him the strength to take charge of his house once more. Even Nefret was more insolent than usual.

She had moved her kittens into his gardening hat. He had searched for it high and low, having forgotten it was in the kitchen cupboard until Mrs. Diggory pointed out the new location of Nefret's nursery with doting pride. The furry brats were too big to stay in it and they were clawing the lining to shreds. He *liked* that hat.

But no one cared about that, not even Miss Snow.

He did wish her mother would go, though he considered Mrs. Snow's devotion to her daughter entirely admirable. But he preferred his life as it had been, with just him and Emma and the children and the servants.

He had other things to worry about, of course. There was much to do before winter set in. The garden needed more plants and the roof needed mending. He would have to go to London and seek Gerald Mixton's advice on his finances. If only he could leave knowing that his houseguests would not be there when he returned . . . but that was not to be.

Lord William could not ask Mrs. Snow to leave without upsetting Emma, just as he could not ask Lady Barbara to leave without insulting his mother. His dear mama had thanked him profusely in her last letter for being so kind to her old friend.

That was another problem. Mrs. Snow and Lady Barbara got along as if they had known each other for a lifetime. The drawing room had become a henhouse. They spent hours in there, cackling away.

Would there be no end to this parade of females?

Apparently not. His brother's latest letter had commended Mrs. Bumpus to his care indefinitely! Edward and Elizabeth were delayed in Cairo, owing to an unforeseen dispute with a superstitious captain who had not wanted a mummy case on his ship. They had decided to book passage on another vessel and precisely when they would return was anyone's guess.

He had caught a glimpse of Mrs. Bumpus an hour ago but had not been in the mood to welcome her and had stayed out of sight.

She had arrived with a great deal of luggage and fanfare, and told the footman to take particular care with the bag that held her medicines. The bottles inside clinked and clanked as Fred carried it upstairs to her bedroom. Possibly she had already planned to stay *as long as she liked*.

And here she was, coming down the stairs. Lord William forced a smile to appear on his lips.

Once on the marble floor of the front hall, Mrs. Bumpus took up the quizzing glass on a chain about her neck and peered at him as if she had never seen him before. "Hello. Where are Caroline and Charles?"

What could he say? That the dear children had swooned with joy over the news of her arrival and were being revived with smelling salts? He knew for a fact that they were hiding in the attic.

"I believe they are, ah, reading with Miss Snow."

She gave a disparaging sniff. "Oh, the village girl. I hope you did not find her uncouth, sir."

"Not at all. She is charming. And quite intelligent."

Mrs. Bumpus looked at him through the quizzing glass again. The lens made one eye appear far larger than the other, a startling effect. "Hm. Then perhaps I will see them at dinner. When do you customarily take your evening repast, Lord William?"

"At six."

She nodded. "I trust the fare will not upset my sensitive digestion. My new doctor gave me highly efficacious pills. I am to take them with meals."

"I will advise the housekeeper accordingly. Bertha can prepare a light dish for you, Mrs. Bumpus." He hoped the cook would not foment a mutiny in the kitchen. Of late Bertha had been swearing loudly enough to be heard upstairs because of the extra work.

"You are exceedingly kind, Lord William. Now, regarding the children—I rather doubt a chit like Miss Snow should be teaching them. I will have to test her knowledge, of course."

"Rest assured that she has done an excellent job in your absence," Lord William began.

The old lady harrumphed. "I shall be the judge of that."

"I see." *No, you will not, you Dreadful Bumpus*, he thought.

"But perhaps the girl will do. My health may prevent me from continuing as their governess."

Had he heard right? Would it be very rude to jump for joy? If Mrs. Bumpus retired, Emma could stay on—well, until Edward and Elizabeth returned. Lord William could not very well justify keeping her here with no children in the house.

Now that he had met her mother, he was not at

all sure that Mrs. Snow would welcome his courtship. She had sized up him and his house quite
quickly and seemed to find them both wanting. It
was all *most* confusing.

"I have had a letter from the children's parents," she began.

"Yes," Lord William sighed. "So have I. Edward's
letter came a few days ago. They have been delayed and he asked if you might stay for a while. So
here you are. What a pleasant surprise."

Mrs. Bumpus managed a semblance of a smile.

"I am glad you think so, sir. Now then. I need a
nap. I always have a nap in the afternoon. My doctor recommends it. If dinner is at six, Winkworth
must wake me at five. Where is he?" She peered
about through the quizzing glass.

Lord William had reached the fraying end of his
patience. She seemed to have no qualms about giving orders to his servants, and, what was worse, saying unkind things about Miss Snow. He was about
to be very rude to her but he shut his mouth just
in time when he saw the butler coming.

Let the imperturbable Wink deal with Mrs.
Bumpus. Lord William had definitely decided upon
the bottle of sherry and a sulk. A walk would not
be enough to cure his irritation.

"Certainly. Here he comes. Ask him anything you
like."

"Winkworth!" she called imperiously. "I must not
miss dinner. You are to arouse me but take care
not to go too far."

The butler clicked his heels and bowed, expres-
sionless. Lord William pressed his lips together,
trying very hard not to laugh and not to look at
Winkworth.

"My nerves will not withstand loud knocks upon the door," she added when neither man spoke.

"Yes, ma'am." They watched the Dreadful Bumpus go back upstairs from whence she had come. "Are more lady guests expected, sir?" the butler asked.

"No, thank God."

"Very good." Winkworth gave him a conspiratorial grin and Lord William felt a little better.

"Have you seen Miss Snow?"

The butler nodded. "I believe that she is in the attic, sir, with the children. They are threatening to run away."

Lord William sighed.

"Caroline and Charlie, you are expected at the table promptly at six. It would be very rude not to greet Mrs. Bumpus."

"If we go in to dinner and say hello nicely, how fast can we leave?" Charlie asked hopefully.

"Not too fast. You must inquire after her health."

"But I know she will say that everything hurts."

"She doesn't like us as you do, Miss Snow," Caroline pointed out. "And she hates cats. What if she tries to drown Nefret's babies?"

Emma was genuinely horrified. "I am sure she would not, Caroline. You must not say such things! Charlie, what have you been telling her?"

He looked pained. "Nothing, Miss Snow."

"I brought the kittens here for safekeeping," Caroline said proudly. She peeked under the cloth covering the basket at her side. "They were in Uncle's hat but there was hardly any room."

"The basket is a better place for them. I think your uncle would like his hat back anyway."

Caroline looked worried. "But they have ruined it."

"I'll buy him a new one with my pocket money," Charles said.

"An excellent idea," Emma said. "He will be pleased and he needs a present. He does not seem happy with so much company in the house."

"Especially Mrs. Bumpus," Charles said.

"Now, now." Emma's tone was gentle.

"At least Mrs. Bumpus will never climb the stairs to the attic," Caroline said. She peeked under the cloth at the kittens again.

"But if Nefret finds out they are here, she will hide them someplace we will never think of," her brother said. "Bring them back to the kitchen, Caro. Mrs. Bumpus will never go there, either."

"Oh, all right." She got to her feet and brushed the dust off her dress.

"That's a good girl." Emma took her hand and picked up the basket. "Come, Charles. You must wash before dinner."

She walked the children downstairs and left them to their ablutions, continuing on with the basket of kittens. As she passed the open door to the library, she heard a growl.

"Come here, Miss Snow," Lord William said gruffly.

Emma entered. He was sitting at his desk, with a bottle of sherry in front of him.

"Yes?"

"Sherry on a empty stomach causes headaches, did you know that?"

"No, sir. I do not drink."

"I find that I have drunk too much, my dear Emma. And I have a very bad headache indeed."

She took a small step back to the door. "How unfortunate."

"Oh, stand still, girl. I will not harm you. I was only hoping that—"

He looked at her miserably, his chin propped on one hand. "I was hoping that there was something to eat in the basket."

"Ah—no. Just the kittens."

The biggest and boldest, with the stripes of his sire, peeked out from underneath the cloth and mewed.

"How sweet," Lord William said sourly. "Perhaps it is hungry as well. I dare say it has a better chance of getting a meal than I do. I seem to have been entirely forgotten, what with all our damned guests and those infernal kittens—"

Emma flashed him an angry look. "My mother is not a 'damned guest' and I will thank you not to refer to her that way."

"I beg your pardon. I meant to say our *esteemed* guests and those infernal kittens."

She turned on her heel to leave. "You are foxed. I will not stay."

"Emma! Forgive me. I am a fool."

She turned back. "I quite agree."

"I wanted to tell you—"

"Yes?"

An odd silence fell between them. Lord William racked his sherry-fogged brain. "I must go to London," he said at last. "I leave tonight."

She stood very straight, not seeming to like that idea very much. What else could he say? He studied her for a long moment. "I will miss you."

Her lips parted with surprise but she did not reply. Hang it all, she and Winkworth and Mrs.

Diggory could manage well enough while he was away. He did have business to transact, and he had to get away.

Sooner or later, he would antagonize her dear mama or squabble with Barbara or the Dreadful B, and there was simply no point. His guests—damned, esteemed, and otherwise—would have to leave eventually. Perhaps when he returned everything would have returned to normal.

"Lord William—" she began.

He held up a hand to silence her. His escape was as good as made. He would not discuss the matter further, and his mixed-up feelings for Miss Snow made it risky for her to remain in the library a second longer. If she did not close her pretty mouth, he would have to kiss her. He waved her away instead.

"Ask Wink to send up a sandwich if you see him," Lord William said. "Ham. Cheese. A bone. Anything to chew on, I don't care."

Emma held her head high and swept out of the library.

He could not get the look she had given him out of his mind. Lord William sat back against the squabs and sighed. The hired coach rattled and shook over the rutted road. He hoped his bags, hastily stowed by Winkworth atop the coach, would not fall off. Still, he could buy anything he needed in London.

He had said good-bye to Caro and Charlie, who seemed somewhat startled by his abrupt departure but did not cry. He had promised to bring something wonderful from London for each. Miss Snow had not said much to him, but chided the children instead in a governessy way.

Well, she *was* their governess. He wondered why it was so easy to forget that.

He planned to bring her back a gift as well but did not say so aloud, since her mother was watching. Still a bit groggy from too much sherry, he imagined presenting Emma with something wildly inappropriate—a diamond bracelet, perhaps, or pearl earbobs. That would give the three hens—Barbara, Bumpus, and Mrs. Snow—something to cluck about.

Of course, he could not afford such baubles, and had no wish to cast the faintest shadow on Emma's spotless reputation. He would bring her back some blameless gift. A dictionary. Or the memoirs of a great and boring man. No one would whisper about those.

Lord William fancied that Emma's mother had given him a sharp look. Did Mrs. Snow suspect that he was in love with her daughter?

A vein in his temple throbbed painfully with each jolt. The road ahead was long. His headache was bound to get worse.

The outskirts of London rolled by in a gray blur. Truly, the city seemed to have grown larger in the few months he had been away. Was that possible? Green fields had been built over and streets cut through pastures where cows had once grazed.

He longed for Devon. He wondered what Caro and Charlie were doing. He missed Emma. He spent the better part of an hour imagining her in every detail. What if she were beside him?

He ought not to fantasize about such things. He looked out the window instead. The coach had gone onto Regent Street and now made a turn, rattling at a breakneck pace through a quiet street.

There was Mixton's house—he recognized it at once. Of gray stone with white trim and a black door, it seemed as respectable as its owner. A handsome red-haired woman peeped out of a window as the coach pulled up.

He recognized her as well—she was Gerald's mistress. Thrifty as always, Gerald kept only one and he kept her close to him, unwilling to pay for a separate apartment. Kitty waved to Lord William, then disappeared from sight.

Gerald's manservant came out and helped the coachman with the bags. Lord William went inside and braced himself for a kiss from Kitty.

She did not keep him waiting long, but burst out of the front room and into the hall, flinging her arms about his neck. He gently disentangled her and returned her affectionate kiss of greeting.

"Here you are at last! Come in and get warm. There is a good fire blazing away in here, but it is smoky—I gave it a poke and a puff from the bellows when I saw you."

She led him into the room she had come from, which was indeed smoky. He coughed.

"Brandy? Port?"

He shook his head. "Nothing for me. I drank an entire bottle of sherry just before I left Devon and I am still feeling the effects."

"Poor thing. But that must have been days ago."

He nodded and unwound his scarf. "It was."

"You never used to drink so much at one go."

"My dear Kitty, I was feeling very sorry for myself at the time. The headache I got made me sorrier still."

Kitty laughed and led him to a chair by the fire. "Wait here. Gerald will soon join us."

She went away and Lord William stretched out, happy to be out of the coach and not at another damned inn. Between the lumpy beds and the noisy customers at the several they'd stopped at, he'd had scarcely a wink of sleep.

But Gerald believed in creature comforts. Lord William knew that a featherbed awaited him. He also knew from his friend's last letter that Gerald had hired an excellent cook, an old Belgian woman who had once run a hotel in Brussels. Lord William looked up as the other man entered the room. His formerly lean friend had become decidedly plump.

Gerald patted his paunch. "What do you think? Should I marry the cook or Kitty?"

Lord William smiled. "Kitty, of course."

"Thank you, m'lud. But Gerald never will and you know it as well as I do," she said tartly.

"Hm. Is the cook pretty?"

Kitty shook her head. "Do you think I would allow another pretty woman in this house?"

"No, I suppose not," Lord William said.

Gerald sat down in another chair and put his slippers onto a footstool. "I expect you've had nothing but mutton pie for days."

"Yes. How did you know?"

Gerald shrugged. "What else is there to eat at an inn?"

"Oh, cheese and beer and such things, all of it bad. The journey is never easy but I am here at last. That is the important thing."

"And why are you here?" Kitty inquired. "We haven't seen you for ever so long, and you sent no letters all summer. Gerald thought you might have fallen in love."

"Hush, Kitty," Gerald said quietly. He did not appear to look at his friend, who looked away in any case.

Lord William was not ready to tell his dear friends about Emma, and he was afraid Kitty would make light of his tender feelings.

The redhead pouted.

"I am here to see to my finances," Lord William began. "I was hoping that Midas Mixton might give me good advice."

Gerald smiled at the use of his nickname. "You have come at the right time. In terms of percentage of returns per annum, I know of investments that would double your—"

Kitty interrupted him with a huge yawn that displayed her fine white teeth. " 'Pon my soul, talk of money makes me feel sleepy."

"It shouldn't," Gerald said.

"Well, it does." She rose and dropped a kiss upon his bald pate. "I think I shall go upstairs and dress properly for dinner."

Gerald watched her flounce out and turned his attention back to Lord William. "As I was saying . . ."

Even after midnight, London was noisy. Yet Lord William had fallen asleep almost immediately after a heavy but delicious meal. A few hours later, his eyes opened. He stirred uneasily, not knowing where he was for several moments, or why he had woken up.

A full moon hung in the sky, filling his room

with a cool blue radiance. He immediately thought
of Emma, knowing that it shone on her, asleep in
her own bed. Ah, if only she dreamed of him as he
did of her . . .

He rolled over but could not get back to sleep.
He looked about the room instead, enjoying its
subdued luxury. The polished wood of the fine
furniture gleamed in the moonlight and so did the
silk draperies at the high window. Gerald had
made a fortune over the years and it showed in this
house.

Lord William vowed to follow his friend's advice
on investing from now on. With the rate of return
Gerald predicted, Lord William would have enough
to rebuild Cranley Hall from the ground up, put
the servants back on full wages, and buy ten thousand rosebushes, for which Jamie would never forgive him.

There would be enough left over to buy Emma
a diamond-studded dress so he could marry her in
the ballroom, which he would restore to its former
grandeur, of course. The ten thousand rosebushes
should provide sufficient flowers for the wedding,
given the right combination of sun and rain.

The weather would simply have to cooperate.

Those were dreams that could very well come
true, even if he would not see the money immediately—possibly not until next spring. Gerald had
been uncharacteristically vague as to the details of
this new investment. Lord William's idle thoughts
drifted to perfectly ridiculous but very amusing
ways to spend his future fortune.

Lady Barbara might be persuaded to leave if he
provided a golden barge rowed by brawny young
men singing her praises. He smiled, imagining her

floating away with those damned peacocks. Mrs. Bumpus could leave with her. He would buy *her* every nostrum, elixir, and patented pill for sale in London if she did. He would even buy her the lifetime services of her very own quack.

His fantasy came to a halt when he thought of Mrs. Snow. The shrewd old lady could not be got rid of so easily. And she was obviously devoted to Emma, her only child and darling daughter.

Lord William sat up in bed. He would have to win Mrs. Snow over somehow. If he married Emma, the old lady might very well come to live with them someday.

Did she want to be a grandmamma? He was not sure. The subject had never come up but then Mrs. Snow had been busy taking care of Emma and making custard.

His own dear mother seemed to enjoy Caro and Charlie but only from a very great distance and only if they were perfectly good.

But the most interesting children were never perfectly good. They brought piglets home. And watched clouds instead of studying. And let kittens sleep in hats that people liked.

He wanted some interesting children of his own. But most of all and first of all, he wanted Emma. . . .

CHAPTER 13

Several hours later and two hundred miles away . . .

Emma walked out shortly after the sun rose, enjoying the autumnal nip in the air. She'd had to escape on the sly, wrapped in the same odd assortment of scarves and shawls that Mrs. Diggory had provided during her convalescence.

Her mother, who had arrived when the weather was still balmy, had not thought to bring Emma's heavy coat or other warm clothes, expecting that she and her daughter would return home before very long.

But. Emma did not mind being dressed like the raggle-taggle gypsy in the old song, so long as she got out of the house. In the days since Lord William's departure, she had quickly grown tired of the exclusive company of women.

Endless cups of tea had been consumed and the same stories told. Lady Barbara's twittering and

Mrs. Bumpus's complaining were equally irritating.

Emma knew more about the insides of the old governess than she wanted to know. The state of Mrs. Bumpus's tetchy liver had been the chief topic of conversation for all of yesterday, and Emma was exceedingly tired of hearing about that troublesome organ.

In the open air, in the pearly light of a clear morning, she might think in peace and walk as long as she liked. She took the path that wound through the fields, soon turning onto another path that would take her up to the crest of a hill.

Charles had once brought her and his sister there in the middle of summer. The three of them had seen the skylarks rising, up and up, wheeling away into the vast sky when they could rise no more. On a clear day, one could catch a glimpse of the distant sea as well.

The wind picked up a bit and the shawl that she had draped over her head and shoulders blew loose. She took the fluttering ends and tied them tightly under her chin, glad that Lord William could not see her in such eccentric attire.

He would be awake by now, she supposed, taking his tea . . . where? She put one foot in front of the other upon the path, wondering if he had gone to the house that his mother shared with his aunt, or if he was staying at a hotel.

No doubt his mama had insisted that he stay with her, as mamas were wont to do. That seemed entirely reasonable and she hoped that was where he was, being properly looked after and fussed over. The thought of Lord William staying anywhere else made Emma feel a trifle jealous.

Still, he was a grown man who had led a life she knew nothing about, traveled abroad, lived in London, and so forth. Emma had only read of such places, and had only gone where her own feet or a light carriage would take her.

Would she ever see more of the world? Beautiful as the Devon countryside was, one could only look at so many hills before wondering what lay on the other side.

The fresh air put a spring in her step and she walked faster, reaching the top of the hill in an hour's time. The view was glorious and she could see the ocean, a distant streak of hazy blue. Closer to home, the crops had been gathered, for the most part, and the trees were brushed with touches of scarlet and gold. Cranley Hall nestled among them.

From here, the house looked exactly like the miniature version that Caroline so loved to play with, perfect in every detail. But its inhabitants were very much alive, coming and going about their usual business.

She could just see white-haired Jamie walking through the garden that he and Lord William had designed together. A moment passed and then a woman joined him. Mrs. Diggory, of course—the old couple often took a brief stroll together when their morning tasks were completed.

Emma smiled. She hoped that their friendship, which was no secret in the household, would blossom into something more.

She looked farther out, over to the outbuildings where the menservants lived, noting one on his way to the stables. Perhaps that was Johnny, who had helped to pull Lord William and Charles from the river on that dreadful day.

It seemed so long ago. The landscape showed no trace of the storm's passing, save for an old oak riven by lightning. It would soon be cut down for firewood.

Another woman—Susie Trelawny, judging by her brisk step, came out the front door with Caroline and Charles. She believed, as Emma did, that children were happier when they were allowed to run and play often.

Susie sat and took out something colorful from the bag she carried—knitting, probably. She was never idle, not for a moment. Another young woman in a white cap came out to talk to her. Molly, most likely, escaping the demands of Lady Barbara. The girl had found out that being a lady's maid was not quite as easy as she thought.

Emma could just hear Caro's faint shriek of laughter as Charlie chased her behind the stone lions that guarded the steps of Cranley Hall.

Was that Mrs. Bumpus peering out the window at them? Perhaps she was feeling better—but Emma had realized that the old lady delighted in giving the appearance of illness, without actually being ill. She was an expert at soliciting sympathy from all who would listen.

Emma fervently hoped never to entertain herself or others with dismal tales of woe. For the most part, she had refused to dwell upon the details of the severe cold she had suffered through and chafed at her status as an invalid.

Still, she was grateful that Caroline and Charles had been so good to her. Everyone had been good, and the ever-cheerful Susie Trelawny had proved to be worth her weight in gold when it came to caring for the children.

Emma had assumed that Mrs. Bumpus would resume their education once more and was surprised when the old governess did not. But Mrs. Bumpus had been in charge of the children for so long, Emma did not want to hurt her feelings by seeming to have taken over entirely during her summer sojourn in Bath.

It seemed the better part of wisdom to let Caroline and Charles enjoy a holiday at home, and not worry about their lessons for the moment. Since Lord William had left Emma with no particular instructions—she had a bottle of sherry to thank for that—she might do as she thought best on their behalf.

Though he had been inebriated, he had to have known that his capable staff would run the house exactly as they had always done. The routines never changed. There was a comforting timelessness about Cranley Hall, which did not seem shabby at all from her vantage point upon the hill.

The old walls, of golden Cotswold stone traced with ivy, glowed warmly in the sun. The great house was a part of the landscape, so much so that it seemed to have stood there always.

She saw Molly go back indoors and Winkworth come out upon the front stairs. He sat down by Susie, who left off knitting and turned to talk to him. Emma wondered what they were saying. Her mother had mentioned something about Winkworth's attentiveness to Susie, come to think of it.

Romance was in the air all around Cranley Hall, evidently, but the man who made Emma's heart beat faster was far away in London. Had he forgotten all about the wonderful kisses they had shared? Perhaps they meant nothing to him. No doubt he had kissed many women before, judging by his tender skill.

So much had happened since the day of the fair. She had come to know him well and her romantic emotions for him had only grown deeper.

She wondered if he would ever stop being such a perfect gentleman and try his luck again. The dramatic rescue of his nephew from the river and the subsequent wild ride on horseback had seemed most promising—and then she had caught cold.

Looking at a red-eyed, sniffling, coughing wretch wrapped in heavy blankets was not the sort of thing that inspired passion in a man. Still, Lord William had been the soul of kindness. He had thought to hire Susie so that Emma might rest; he had summoned her mother when Emma did not improve.

She had been glad enough to see Mama, but perhaps she ought not to have confided her tender feelings, however shrewdly her mother had guessed at them. Following Mama's offhand advice to ignore Lord William had not worked out at all.

Emma turned her face to the sun, basking in its meager warmth. She drew her warm things more tightly around herself, closed her eyes and imagined him kissing her upon his return from London.

If no one was watching, she would run into his strong arms . . . let him sweep her off her feet . . . and she would respond, body and soul. *How romantic*, as little Caroline liked to say.

Not that it would ever happen. She opened her eyes and sighed. To ease her frustration, she kicked a loose stone down the hill. It tumbled in the general direction of Cranley Hall, bounced off another stone, and disappeared into the tops of the trees below.

With so many people in the house, two of whom he heartily disliked, Lord William was likely to disappear into his library once he had said hello to Caroline and Charles, and busy himself with various projects.

She knew him well enough to predict what he might do first upon his return to Cranley Hall. He would discuss the household accounts with Mrs. Diggory and the improvements to the garden with Jamie Crichton, ask Winkworth if any ceilings had fallen down during his absence or whether the roof had sprung new leaks. Then he would inquire politely as to Emma's health and the progress of the children's education.

She had a few questions of her own on that subject. Who would be governess when Caroline and Charlie's parents returned? It might seem self-serving if Emma made a point of saying that Mrs. Bumpus was more interested in her health than the children these days. Of course, she would not put it in quite those words.

The faint sound of their laughter reached her on the wind, and Emma's heart lifted. Everything would come right in time—and Lord William would come home soon enough.

She went around a clump of bushes to find the path, and stopped to look at Cranley Hall one last time. From here she could just see the ballroom behind the house. It looked much less like a beehive from up high—its round roof was not covered with ivy. Now that summer's lush greenery had died back, the outlines of old flowerbeds around it were clearly visible.

What a pretty place it must have been. Surely the ballroom's eventual restoration was on Lord William's long list of things to do . . . somewhere near the bottom. The Cranley Hall roof was first.

She began to walk down, hoping that his business in London would prove profitable—and that he would soon return.

Lord William entered the coffee-house two steps behind Gerald, who swaggered in as if he owned the place. His friend was greeted by other customers as if he did.

It was here that Gerald had begun to build his fortune, simply by listening to the swirl of talk about stocks and shares and such, and making singularly clever investments with the small capital he possessed. The man had doubled his money time after time.

They slid into a booth and the proprietress came over. She smiled broadly and bent low to wipe the table with a filthy rag, displaying a wealth of freckled bosom. "If it ain't Midas Mixton. Who's yer friend?"

"This is—ah—Mr. Kent."

"Ooh. He's a handsome one." She gave William's side of the table an extra swipe. "I am glad to have the pleasure of your acquaintance, Mr. Kent."

Gerald looked up at her. "Two coffees, Peggy, if you please. We shall be staying a while."

She nodded and eyed Lord William again. "Fancy a muffin on the side, sir?"

He was not sure whether she was offering a bit
of breakfast or herself. Gerald grinned. "Have one.
Peggy bakes them on the premises when she is not
flirting with the customers. They are really quite
good."

She snapped the rag at his paunch. "Ye don't
need a muffin, Gerry boy."

"Oh, why not? Bring two. And plenty of butter.
And a plate of sliced ham while you're at it."

"Anyfing else?"

"That will be all. For now."

Peggy nodded and sidled away, pausing to chat
with another man who had just come in. He was
talking fast and only stopped to draw breath when
he saw Gerald.

The man dashed over. "Mixton! Today is my lucky
day! I have a golden opportunity indeed if you
have a minute to listen—"

Gerald waved him away. "Do not waste my time,
man."

Peggy took the fellow by the arm and led him
elsewhere in the coffee-house.

Gerald sighed. "I am too well-known, Will. I am
offered such opportunities all the time. Most are
not worth the time it takes to explain them. And in
truth, I have done so well in the last six months
that I do not need more 'opportunities.' "

"So why do you come here?" Lord William looked
about at the dingy room, which smelled unpleas-
antly of stale tobacco. For a few pence, one could
order a pipe and smoke for hours. He thought of
his failed investment in the Virginia plantation and
sighed. He did not have his friend's rare gift for
making money.

Gerald leaned forward. The small mullioned

window above their table cast a weak light upon his bald head. He looked, incongruously, like a medieval saint. "I am madly in love with Peggy," he whispered.

"What?" Lord William cast a quick glance at the proprietress's homely face. "That cannot be, not when you have Kitty to warm your bed," Lord William whispered back.

"But she cannot snap a rag like Peggy. Makes my blood runs hot!" He sat up straight and laughed uproariously, slapping the table. "Had you there for one second, didn't I?"

"You did."

Gerald looked about again. "I come here simply to listen, as I always have. One learns much more that way, you know."

Though it was not yet noon, the coffee-house was nearly full. Peggy moved about, passing out a newspaper here and a pipe there, and seeing that everyone had their coffee or tea. The hubbub of deal-making, trading, and business gossip had already reached a high pitch.

Lord William shook his head. "I could listen to these fellows for twenty years and still not understand most of what they say."

"That is why you have me, Will. I am happy to interpret."

Peggy came over with a mug of coffee in each hand, and two muffins cradled in the crook of her arm. She set down the mugs and caught the muffins as they rolled down her sleeve, setting one at each side of the table with a flourish.

"A neat trick, Peg. Tell Mr. Kent where you used to work."

She guffawed. "Drury Lane Theatre, jugglin' during the interval."

"I see," said Lord William. "But I will take a plate, if you don't mind."

"And bring one for me, Peggy."

"The gen'l'man in the booth behind is a'most finished with his."

"I want my own plate—a clean one. So does Mr. Kent."

She grinned broadly. "O'course." She walked away again and came back with the ham, a little crock of butter that had been smoothed out between customers, though telltale crumbs remained, and several small plates. She took knives and forks from her apron pocket and set them upon the table, adding serviettes almost as an afterthought.

"Thank you," Gerald said. He tucked into the food, but continued to talk—mostly gibberish about turning straw into gold and how the world could be spun on a shilling when the time was right.

Lord William ate but with little appetite. The dingy coffee-house was a far cry from the sunny room where he took breakfast with Miss Snow and the children. He missed her terribly.

Peggy sauntered by again with a full coffeepot. "More, Mr. Kent? Anyfing else for you, Mr. Mixton?"

"I believe I will have more of that ham, Peggy."

"Very good, sir."

"Nothing for me, thank you." Lord William took a last bite of his muffin and finished his coffee. "Now tell me again exactly what is it I am investing in, Gerald."

"A mine."

"What sort of mine?"

Gerald waved his butter knife in the air. "A minor detail. Ha ha. A feeble joke—forgive me, Will."

Lord William rolled his eyes. "Not unless you tell me what I want to know."

"Oh, very well. It is a coal mine, of course. But it has not been worked for years. The shaft filled up with water a week after it was drilled and no one has ever figured out how to drain it. The shaft is very deep, and the vein of ore is deeper still."

Lord William gave him a narrow look. "So why would I want to invest in it?"

"It is cheap. Who would buy shares of a flooded mine but a madman?"

"That would be you."

"And you as well. You entrusted me with a thousand pounds and you stand to make a killing. When my wild-eyed Scotsman perfects his astonishing machine, the mine will be worth millions of pounds."

"Wait a minute. You said nothing about a wild-eyed Scotsman last night. Or an astonishing machine."

"Did I not mention Mr. McNair and his steam engine? I thought I had. Thank you, m'dear." Gerald attacked the fresh piece of ham that Peggy set in front of him.

"No."

"McNair has invented the steam engine to end all steam engines. He claims it can drain a flooded mine in a day."

"Have you seen any proof?"

Gerald chewed and swallowed. "His machine is more powerful than any other. The first one he built blew him sky-high when it got going. But he survived. Landed in a cow pasture. Now he has a new one, with rather better engineering in all its parts. "

"I see," said Lord William. "Do go on."

"He is a brilliant fellow, for all his eccentricity."

Lord William shrugged. "I have a wild-eyed Scotsman working for me as well. But he is a gardener."

"Well, McNair is a genius. I have invested in his steam engine as well as the mine. He has a manufacturer ready to build hundreds more; and a company to ship them all over the world. Mines are always flooding, you know."

"Yes, of course," said Lord William irritably. He knew absolutely nothing about mines.

"If our mine can be drained, your thousand pounds will become a great fortune. You will be rich and I will be . . . even richer."

The coffee-house suddenly became deathly still. All motion ceased and all eyes were on them. Gerald looked around at the sea of faces. "Had you there for a minute, didn't I, fellows?" He laughed uproariously again.

Peggy let out a hoot, but the habitués of the coffee-house looked stricken and sad, as if something infinitely precious had been dangled in front of them and then snatched away. Gerald sat there and rubbed his hands with glee. "Everyone knows McNair is insane. Isn't that right, Mr. Kent?"

"Quite."

CHAPTER 15

Gerald tossed a few coins onto the scarred table, and they took their leave of Peggy. Lord William was glad to get out of the tobacco-smelling fug of the coffee-house.

The street was crowded with passers-by, who shouldered their way past. Gerald walked briskly, not looking behind him. For all that he was much taller, Lord William found it difficult to keep up. Conversation was impossible.

They reached the embankment of the Thames after several minutes, where Gerald, winded, sat on the marble wall of someone's riverside house. He pulled out a handkerchief and mopped his brow.

"Are you afraid they will come after you? It was only a joke, Gerald. At their expense, of course. But nothing worth fighting over."

"Maybe. Maybe not." Gerald took deep breaths.

"So tell me. Where did you really put my thousand pounds and what rate of return should I expect? Three percent? Four?"

Gerald shook his head. "I told you. I invested your money in the derelict mine and McNair's steam engine. It was foolish of me to mention it in a coffee-house but I did not realize that everyone was listening, despite the noise."

"Good God. Do you mean that bizarre tale was true?"

"Every word."

Lord William sat down beside him on the wall and folded his arms over his chest. "Hm. The investment is speculative."

"Yes. But McNair is already assembling his new machine at the colliery. It is located on the border of Wales. We can get there in time if we leave today. Do come with me."

Lord William stood up again and paced. "I was going to visit Mama."

"For weak tea and little cakes? Visit your mama some other time. Please come with me. At least my Scotsman will bring a bottle of whisky."

"For all I know, his machine is powered by it," Lord William grinned. "Very well, Gerald. I have to trust you. I have no choice. You have my money."

Gerald nodded. "Yes. I haven't touched it, you know. Put up my own. If the steam engine fails, you lose nothing. And if it doesn't—as I said, you will be rich and I will be richer. A thousand pounds is not much money to me."

"What?" Lord William cried. "It is to me—and it is mine. I had only hoped to earn enough on it to fix my damned roof—I do not want your charity, Gerald!"

His friend gave him a look of mild reproof. "I can invest it elsewhere if you like, in a fund suitable for widows and orphans. In the meantime, it is safely tucked away in a box at the Bank of England."

Lord William scarcely knew what to do or say. He decided to pace faster. Up and down. Up and down. Gerald watched him with a smile.

"Don't wear out the stones, Will. Everything happens for the best."

"Does it?" Lord William shook his head. "This has been the strangest summer of my life. First Miss Snow, and now this."

Gerald's eyebrows rose. "Who is Miss Snow? You did not mention her last night."

"And you did not mention McNair, however much you try to make me believe you did."

"You are dodging my question. Who is Miss Snow?"

"Caro and Charlie's governess."

Gerald grinned rather wolfishly. "I see. Is she pretty?"

"Very."

"Is she sweet?"

"Yes."

"Is she quiet and shy?"

"Not at all. She is spirited—and fearless."

Gerald rose and slapped him on the back. "And you are in love. It was bound to happen sooner or later."

"I did not say I was in love, Gerald," Lord William protested.

"It is obvious. You are a fool but congratulations anyway."

"And I thought you cared for nothing but money."

Gerald shook his head. "Ah, no. I am a romantic man in my way. Ask Kitty."

"I would rather not."

"You can tell me all about Miss Snow on the way to Wales. I wonder where we might hire that coach. We must have it exclusively, of course. What if I talk in my sleep? The driver will want to buy shares of McNair's machine and soon the whole world will want to get in on it."

"You talk too much when you are awake, Gerald."

His friend laughed gleefully. "Too true."

Much later that night, Lord William found himself inside a hired coach for the second time in two days. Gerald had gone promptly to sleep but William could not. They banged and jolted over rutted roads in utter darkness. The border was many hours away and he had plenty of time to think about his wonderful new investment.

Of course, all he thought about was Miss Snow.

CHAPTER 16

The yawning opening that led to the coal mine was, well, black as coal. Lord William looked at it uneasily. He felt nothing but sympathy for the miners who went down into pits like it every day of their short lives, slaving away for a few shillings a week.

A coal mine was a hellish place. But if this could be opened again and he realized the extraordinary return on his investment that Gerald promised, he would endeavor, as one of two majority owners, to pay decent wages and do whatever good he could otherwise.

If Gerald insisted on profit above all, Lord William would persuade him to be more humane. If Gerald could not be persuaded, Lord William would simply bully him.

He watched Fergus McNair clamber up to make last-minute adjustments to his steam engine. This was connected to pipes and pumps and channels that supposedly would drain millions of gallons of water from the pit.

Lord William doubted it. But Gerald seemed to have great faith in the Scotsman and his invention. He had taken pains to explain that a steam engine was nothing new—even a dreamer like Will ought to know that.

He went on to say that it was the power this one generated that made it different, the precision of its manufacture, the careful fitting of its ingenious pistons to its cylinders, and so forth.

McNair had chimed in, explaining precisely how he had improved upon the designs of the great James Watt, his countryman, in a burr too thick for Lord William to understand.

Gerald seemed to grasp the engineering part of it, if not McNair's actual words. Lord William supposed that was enough. The design of a machine could be clearly understood from a diagram.

He walked away from the gaping maw of the mine, looking for a place to sit down. Everything in sight was blackened by coal dust. No flowers grew, and no grass. In the valley far below he saw snug little homes, nestled together as if they found safety in numbers against the flank of the solitary, brooding mountain that held the coal.

He shook his head. The men who might work here would come from that village. He felt a flash of guilt. Cranley Hall was heated by coal—yet he had never thought about where it came from.

He vowed again to dedicate a goodly share of his profits to the men who toiled to wrest the coal from the mountain. Of course, his noble gesture might never have to be made.

McNair's machine could not pump out an underground river. The geologist that Gerald had hired said as much. Mr. Streatham, the mine's former owner, a plainspoken, rough-hewn man who seemed to be made of rock himself, agreed with the geologist.

As usual, Gerald agreed with no one except McNair, whom he barely understood. The geologist kept busy poking about in the rubble, picking up a piece of stone now and then to study. The mine's former owner folded his arms across his vast chest and watched McNair tinker with his machine.

The Scotsman's assistants tightened things, or loosened things, and muttered to each other in Gaelic. Lord William knew a few words of it, thanks to Jamie. The long and the short of it: they were cursing.

Hours went by. At last all was ready. McNair gave the signal and the many parts of his machine began to move, slowly at first and then faster, and faster still. Gerald ran over to the huge pipe, positioned so that the pumped water would flow into a narrow crevasse in the rock and down the mountain, well away from the village.

He straddled it and hung his head over the top of it to look inside.

"Arr ye daft?" McNair yelled.

"Gerald! When the water comes, you will be swept away!" Lord William called.

"But there is no water. McNair, your machine does not work. Did you not say it would flow immediately?"

"Aye! Move, ye bluidy fool!"

Gerald jumped off the pipe. A great rumbling

shook the ground and water blasted out with tremendous force only seconds later. The men stood by and marveled.

McNair screamed with wild joy.

Hours later, it was still running.

The sun set. The moon rose. The men took shelter in the foreman's tumbledown hut and slept on the floor. The moon set. The sun rose.

The water ran on. The question was—how much was left inside? The quantity of water coming from the pipe did not seem to have diminished.

Mr. Streatham explained the working of the winch chain, and platform by which a man or two might be let down hundreds of feet into the dark shaft, carrying a lantern. "I will go. I am the only one here who knows how high the water was."

"I will go with you," the geologist said. "My curiosity compels me, though it is hardly safe."

Gerald smiled. "Well, that makes two and you said it takes two, Mr. Streatham. So Lord William and I will wait here with McNair and the other men."

With no further ado, Mr. Streatham and the geologist climbed into a sort of bucket. Two of McNair's men worked the winch that let them down.

Lord William suppressed a shudder. They were braver than he was by far. After what seemed too long a time, the men on the mountain heard a distant shout from inside it. "Hoi!"

He breathed a sigh of relief when they appeared again.

"What did you see?" Gerald asked eagerly. "Is the water any lower?"

Mr. Streatham stepped onto the black dust and spat. "No. It is the same. The mine cannot be drained."

"But—but—" Gerald looked over at the gushing pipe.

The geologist shook his head. "The vein is close to an underground river. If you ran McNair's machine for a thousand years or more, you could not drain it."

"Damnation!" That was Gerald.

"But ma machine works!" That was McNair, proudly patting his contraption.

Gerald snapped out of his fit of temper in a flash. "Why, so it does. There you go, Will. I expect we shall turn a profit after all. How much of it do we own, Mr. McNair?"

"I fergit."

"A good thing I wrote it all down and had you sign it, McNair." He turned to the others and spoke in a louder voice. "Gentlemen, you are witness to a historic moment. When capital meets genius, the result is profit. Heaps of profit. The first shares of McNair-Mixton Mining will be offered upon our triumphant return to London." He put an arm around the Scotsman's shoulders, as if they were posing for a mural in a government building. McNair scowled.

Weary from their night on a rough floor, sooty-faced and filthy, the group just stared at Gerald. Lord William spoke first. "I think I speak for everyone when I say hurrah and all that. But I am going home to Cranley Hall."

He turned and walked down the mountain.

* * *

Lord William stopped in London first, however, to see his mother. It meant going the long way round—the road to Devon was close to the border of Wales—but Mama would be deeply hurt if she should learn that he had been to the city but not to her house.

As Gerald had predicted, she served him weak tea and little cakes. She seemed much the same, as quiet as always.

"My dear Will. It is so good of you to visit. I wish you could come to London more often."

"I wanted to see you, Mama. And I had financial matters to attend to. Gerald Mixton advised me how best to invest the money Papa sent and I have done. I shall be able to repair Cranley Hall. Of course, if you need anything, let me know at once. My solicitors can make a deposit in your account."

"Thank you, dear." His mother's brow furrowed slightly. "I remember Gerald. Wasn't he the boy from Mixton Grange who taught you to play cards and won all your pocket money? He was bad even then. I wish you would not associate with such people, William."

"His character has improved greatly since that dark day, Mama."

She smiled at him. "Then I shall not worry. By the bye, how is my friend Barbara? Has she enjoyed her stay at Cranley Hall?"

Lord William coughed. "I—I expect she has." He gulped the rest of his tea.

"She is a funny old thing. We were childhood friends . . . but I told you that. Oh, dear, I am repeating myself. I expect Barbara and I both qualify as funny old things by now."

"Never, Mama. You look younger than ever."

"Piffle. More tea?"

He could see she was pleased. Her wrinkled cheeks turned faintly pink. "Yes, thank you." He held out his cup.

"Barbara will stay forever, you know. You cannot be overly tactful. Your brother simply locks himself in his study when she comes."

Lord William took another small cake and ate it whole. His gentle mother seldom spoke with such bluntness.

"So Charlie said."

"I miss my grandchildren."

"Shall I bring them to London? They are past the stage of breaking things and they even listen sometimes. Miss Snow has done wonders with them."

His mother nodded. "Edward mentioned her. He hoped that—" She broke off.

"Yes?"

"Oh, nothing. I believe that he is returning at last. I had a letter only yesterday."

"Then you have heard from him much more recently than I. What does he say?"

She rose and went over to a small desk, unlocked it, and withdrew a letter in his brother's familiar hand. "Is this it? I have misplaced my spectacles." She gave it to him.

"Yes. I will help you find them in a moment, Mama." He set down his teacup and read the letter silently.

Dear Mama,
Elizabeth and I shall return upon The Suez, though precisely when we shall arrive in London, I cannot say. We leave on the morrow.

Edward had written the day's date at the top of the letter, William noted. He continued to read.

Our voyage will take several weeks, as The Suez calls at several Mediterranean ports. But the captain is an Englishman, a broad-minded, enlightened fellow with an avid interest in antiquities—unlike the last, who refused to carry certain of our souvenirs.

The mummy case, of course.

Elizabeth and I look forward with great joy to seeing the children as soon as we arrive. Perhaps you could persuade William to bring them to London.

"Edward asks if I may bring the children to London."

"Of course. That will work out nicely," his mother said. "Everyone can stay with me. It has been a long time since our family filled a pew at the church. Your father, old reprobate that he is, avoided churches like the plague—but never mind that. I have forgiven him for everything except that dreadful Frenchwoman. But then she has to live with your father, and I suppose that is punishment enough for the likes of her."

William looked at her curiously. There was nothing he could think of to say to that. "Thank you, Mama. May I bring Caro and Charlie's governess?"

She nodded. "I should like to meet her. Your brother and his wife hold her in high regard."

"With good reason." William folded up the letter and thought for a moment. He could go back to Devon for Emma and Caro and Charlie, even stay there for a little while, perhaps a week or more, and return to London in time to meet his brother and sister-in-law.

Edward and Elizabeth would have to resolve the question of Mrs. Bumpus themselves, but he was damned if he would travel with the woman. She could stay where she was. Mrs. Snow could go back to her husband. Lady Barbara—well, he would figure out what to do about her when he got back to Cranley Hall. He felt as if he had been away too long.

Lord William rose to leave. "As you say, it will all work out nicely. Good-bye, Mama."

"Good-bye, dear boy. Give everyone my fondest love. I am looking forward to the great reunion!"

CHAPTER 17

Meanwhile, back at Cranley Hall . . .

Nefret's kittens were big enough to give away. She crouched under the library sofa to watch the proceedings, her tail twitching. Caroline solemnly presented Jamie with a striped one.

"Here you are, Mr. Crichton."

"Och, he is feisty." He let the kitten scramble up the rough material of his shirt and sit on his shoulder. "What shall his name be, lass?"

"You may name him. He is your cat."

Jamie thought it over. "MacKenzie. That is easy to remember."

"We can call him Mack for short. That is even easier," Charlie said.

"That it is, lad. Yer name is Mack," he said to the kitten. It settled down near Jamie's ear and purred loudly.

Caroline picked up the only kitten that looked

like Nefret. "Mrs. Diggory, you asked for this one. She is just like her mother."

"Aye, golden eyes and all," Jamie said. "And a verra wicked look she has."

"She is not at all wicked," Caroline said indignantly, giving the sand-colored kitten to Mrs. Diggory.

"I shall call her—oh, I don't know. Would you like to name this one, miss, since your brother named Mack?"

The little girl stroked the kitten's head. It seemed quite at home in Mrs. Diggory's lap. "Miss Snow can name her. I can't think of anything."

"Cleopatra," Emma said.

"I have it! Cleo*catr*a!" Charlie said.

"Charlie, no." But Emma laughed all the same.

"Cleo is a nice short name," Mrs. Diggory said. "What do you think, miss?"

"Cleo rhymes with Caro. I like it," Caroline said.

"Then this one is Cleo," Emma said. "Who is next? Only two left. Beautiful cats, free of charge." She looked around the library at everyone gathered there.

Susie stepped forward. "I will have that one, miss. Our Blimey is getting old and this little fellow will be his father's pride and joy."

"You can call him Blimey Two," said Charlie.

She shook her head. "That is too long and too grand a name for a tavern cat. I need to yell it at him if he gets in the cream, Charlie," Susie said.

"Call him Blue then," the butler suggested.

"Blue! Oh, that is perfect." Susie cuddled her kitten in her arms under Winkworth's approving gaze. "Yer name is Blue. How d'ye like that?"

"One kitten left," Emma said. "One fine, fat kitten."

"That one is yours, Miss Snow," Caroline said suddenly. "You can take him with you when you go."

Tears came to Emma's eyes. "Oh—I never want to leave Cranley Hall."

Caroline looked concerned. "But your mama has gone home and she will miss you if you stay here."

Emma sighed. "I suppose you are right. I would be happy to take the last kitten. Do you approve, Nefret?"

The cat yawned.

"What shall I call him, Caroline?"

"Name him after Mr. Winkworth," Susie said, flashing the butler an impudent look. "Call him Wink for short."

"I would consider myself honored." Winkworth made a sweeping bow.

"Wink it is!" Emma said, feeling a bit more cheerful.

Caroline sighed with pleasure, her job done. "Now that the kittens have been distributed, may we play in the front hall, Miss Snow? Uncle is coming home tonight."

"Snow is falling—not much but a little. The roads are slippery and his carriage might be delayed. But you may stay up for a little while. He might come tonight after all."

"Thank you, Miss Snow." She took Charlie's hand and the children left the library.

"Shall we walk outside and look at the snow, Wink?" Susie said.

"Yes, my dear. You do not mind, do you, Miss Snow?"

"Not at all."

"I think I will have a wee drop of whisky in the kitchen. Mary, would ye care to imbibe?"

"Certainly not. But I will go with you, Jamie. Please excuse us, Miss Snow."

The old couple left too, and Emma was all alone—no, not quite. Nefret jumped up into her lap and hissed at a kitten that tried to follow. She accepted Emma's gentle stroking with a gracious bend of her neck. "There, there. Settle down."

But Nefret's ears pricked at a noise only she could hear.

"What is it?"

Emma turned her head toward the window but the light snow outside seemed to muffle the usual night noises. She strained to listen.

There it was—wheels. Carriage wheels. Coming closer. Lord William was home at last.

Caroline and Charlie opened the front door, startled to see Winkworth on the other side of it with Susie.

"You're supposed to be in here, Wink. What are you doing?"

"Never you mind. I think your uncle has come back." Winkworth let Susie Trelawny go in ahead of him and then came in, standing to one side of the open door in his usual place.

Caroline peered out into the snow. "I can't see!"

A black hired coach rumbled into view and pulled up between the stone lions that guarded the stairs.

Lord William swung open the door and jumped out without waiting for the coachman.

"Uncle!" Charlie yelled. He ran outside but Susie hung on to Caroline.

"Hello, Charlie!" He took his nephew's hand and ran up the stairs. Caroline wrapped herself around his legs. "Uncle uncle uncle! Uncle uncle uncle!"

He laughed and picked her up. "No one has ever been so happy to see me, Caro!" He looked up to see Emma coming down the stairs, her face aglow.

"Welcome home," she said softly.

"I am very glad to be here, Miss Snow." He could not take his eyes from hers. He had been away for three weeks, missing her all the while—and there she was, just as he remembered her. Doe eyes. Honey-colored hair tied up with an artless ribbon. Pink cheeks. Soft gown. No, no, he was quite wrong—Emma was much lovelier than he remembered. To see her look so happy, as if she had been waiting for him all this time, made his heart swell with joy.

But he had much to attend to before he could talk to her. The rest of the servants appeared, running to bring in his bags and let the coachman drive off before it began to snow in earnest. Everyone talked at once.

"Welcome, Lord William!"

"You must be weary—let me take your coat."

"Did you bring me something?" a little voice said right in his ear.

"Yes, Caro!" He set her down. "It is in the valise. Let me take it out. It is fragile and you must handle it carefully."

She ran to the bag and brought it to him. "What is it?"

"Something very nice." He rummaged inside and pulled out a lumpy object wrapped in one of his neck cloths. He let her unwrap it. A miniature piano of gold-painted wood appeared. "It is for your dollhouse. It is a music box. Wind the key underneath—here, let me do it. You must not overwind it, Caro." He took the little piano from her and showed her how.

A tiny, sparkling melody filled the air.

Emma recognized it. Mozart. How charming! What a wonderful gift for a little girl.

"Thank you, Uncle William! It is beautiful!"

He waved Charlie over. "Look in the other bag. Don't worry. You can't break your gift. Do be careful not to drop it on your foot."

Charlie unclasped the bag his uncle pointed to and pulled out an immense book. He shouted with joy. "What I wanted!"

"Not a piglet, but it will do, eh?" Lord William laughed. "It is a comprehensive natural history. Everything from aardvarks to zebus, my boy."

"Thank you, Uncle!"

"We missed you so much," Caroline said, more softly.

"Why were you gone so long?"

"I had to see my friend Gerald—straighten out my financial affairs. I am happy to report that I now own shares in a steam engine. Part of a steam engine, anyway."

"Which part?" Charlie asked. "I would like to build a steam engine."

"The part that makes money. I almost became

part owner of a coal mine too, but it was flooded and the steam engine could not pump out all the water—oh, it is a long, long story. I will tell you all about it later. But it seems that there will be more money coming in than I hoped for. Which means that I can once again pay full wages."

Lord William straightened, looking around the circle of servants and again at Emma, who still stood upon the very bottom stair. Some of the faces he had expected to see were not there.

"Where have our esteemed guests gone? Are they abed? Well, it is late—I hope I have not disturbed them."

"Lady Barbara has gone to Venice to live in a palazzo," Caroline began. "And she is looking forward to traveling in a gondola to do her shopping, Uncle."

So his fantasy of Lady Barbara floating away and out of his life had not been too far off the mark, Lord William thought. Interesting.

"She will be a companion to a contessa," Charlie added.

"I see. Well, I am sure that we will all miss her." There was a moment of silence. No one seemed to know how to respond politely to that statement. "But we will have the peacocks to remind us of her," he added brightly.

"She took the peacocks, sir," Winkworth said.

"Certainly no one will miss *them*. What wonderful news! I am very happy for Lady Barbara. And where is Mrs. Bumpus?"

"She ran away with her new doctor," Mrs. Diggory said.

"You are joking."

"It is true," Emma said, laughing.

"And where is your mother, Miss Snow? Surely she did not leave as well."

"My father insisted that she come home."

Lord William nodded, not wishing to seem too happy that his future mother-in-law was no longer at Cranley Hall. He had made up his mind on the way home, of course. There would be no more plans, no more schemes, and no more worrying about whether one course of action was more respectable than another. Emma had to marry him and that was that.

Mrs. Snow might return whenever she wished. Cranley Hall was Emma's home—and he was going to become Emma's husband as soon as possible.

He looked around at the beaming faces in the hall once more. Everyone seemed to have paired off somehow.

"This looks like the end of a play," he said.

"What do you mean, sir?" asked Mrs. Diggory. She made no effort to remove Jamie Crichton's arm, which was firmly wrapped about her round middle.

Lord William noticed Winkworth's hands at the side of Susie's slender waist. As if no one would notice. "I mean that each man has found his maid. Soon you will all be skipping around and talking in rhyming couplets. What has been going on?"

Susie dimpled very prettily. "Nothing at all."

"Hm."

Caroline and Charlie took advantage of the lull in the conversation to besiege their uncle with hugs once more. He hugged them back, one at a time. "I have an even better present but it is for both of you. Your parents are on a ship and are sailing home from Egypt. They will be in England by Christmas!"

Caroline burst into tears. "Mama! I want my mama!"

He soothed her and Charlie whipped out a handkerchief. "Here, Caro."

She looked at it through her tears and shook her head. "It is not very clean, Charlie." Just the thought of being presented with such an object made her lip tremble. Caroline seemed on the verge of fresh howls.

Lord William picked her up. "Charlie meant well. Now don't cry, Caro. This is a happy occasion!"

Emma patted the little girl on the back. "There, there. Christmas will be here sooner than you think."

Caroline indulged herself in one last prodigious sniff and Lord William set her down. "But I miss them now. What shall we do until then?" she asked sadly.

"We are going to go to London to visit your grandmamma and stay with her until your parents come," Lord William began. "We can see the pantomimes at Drury Lane and wander 'round the best toy stores and we might even pay a visit to the Duke of Snook and his world-famous menagerie."

"Is there a Duke of Snook? I have never heard of him," Charlie said.

"Of course not. Consider yourself snookered, Charles."

The boy looked embarrassed.

"But your grandmamma is a countess and she probably does know a duke or two. One of them is bound to have a menagerie."

"You are teasing me, Uncle."

"No. There are many strange animals to be found in London. It's all a question of knowing where to look. Miss Snow will come with us—if she wants to, that is. And Susie too. Can you spare Susie for a few weeks, Wink?"

Wink sighed. "If I must."

"Would you like to go, Miss Snow?" He gave Emma a pleading look—his very best, bright-eyed, no-woman-shall-resist-this pleading look.

"More than anything."

"That's settled, then." He turned to the house-keeper. "My dear Mrs. Diggory, I find that I am famished. Do you think that you could persuade Bertha to fix a light supper?"

"No, sir."

"Why not?"

"Bertha gave notice and left with Lady Barbara. She said she always wanted to go to Italy."

"Oh! How interesting. I suppose there is bread and cheese in the pantry—and there must be some sherry in the house."

Winkworth raised an eyebrow. "In the library, sir."

"Excellent. I shall eat in the library, if Mrs. Diggory will permit such liberties."

Mrs. Diggory gave him a puzzled look. "Sir, it is not my place to tell you yea or nay."

"Even better. Than you will not object if Miss Snow joins me."

Everybody's eyebrows went up. Lord William mentally counted fourteen raised eyebrows in all. He gave Winkworth his cloak and heavy coat, and offered his arm to Miss Snow. "Shall we?"

Emma looked at Mrs. Diggory, who gave her a barely perceptible nod. Winkworth motioned to Charlie to stay put and Susie took Caro's hand.

Emma took Lord William's arm and they went up the stairs together.

"Thank you, Winkworth."

Lord William watched the butler set the supper tray upon his desk. Winkworth looked over at Emma, who was sitting rather primly on the sofa, and smiled. "Will there be anything else, sir?"

"No."

The butler bowed and withdrew. Lord William ignored the tray and the food upon it, but did not say why. He stood there in silence, looking thoughtfully at her, which made her very nervous.

"Well, I cannot tell you that your supper is getting cold, because it is already cold, Lord William," Emma said.

He nodded, and began to pace the room, his hands clasped behind his back. "I suppose you are wondering why I wished to see you. I am not really hungry—the bread and cheese was for the sake of propriety, so that a servant might enter from time to time. But I do wish Mrs. Diggory had sent up a pie. A piece of pie would be very nice."

She looked at him pertly. "Is a pie more proper, then?"

Lord William grinned at her. "Not the way you eat one, my dear." He could not help but remember their outing in the rowboat and how she had retrieved a flaky bit of piecrust from her bosom. But then, she had not known that he had witnessed her amusing lapse of manners, and it would not do to explain it all in great detail. Besides, he had other things that he wanted to talk to her about.

"I beg your pardon?"

"Miss Snow," he began, then stopped himself mid-sentence. He stopped pacing as well. "I had a most interesting time in London. I wish I had been able to write to you and the children, but of course, I was not always in London, as my dear friend Gerald Mixton saw fit to drag me to an abandoned coal mine in Wales."

"Oh, dear. Not for a picnic, surely. It sounds dangerous."

"I assure you, though the mine was hundreds of feet deep and awash in black water, I myself was in no danger—" He stopped again, realizing that she was teasing him. Perhaps Emma was piqued by his long absence. That was understandable. Should he tell her how much he had missed her? No, no. Explanations first. Then the sweet nothings.

Emma smiled up at him radiantly as he walked over to the sofa where she sat.

"Gerald wanted me to invest in a wondrous machine devised to pump water from flooded mines. The inventor, a Mr. McNair, was testing it for the first time."

"I see," Emma said. "Did it work?"

"Yes. Quite well, in fact. But the mine proved to be connected to an underground river, so it will have to stay flooded. But Gerald says McNair's machine will make us rich. Somewhat rich. Perhaps I should say less poor. He intends to form a company—McNair-Mixton Mining—or is it Mixton-McNair Mining? I cannot remember and in any case it does not matter."

"I hope that the endeavor succeeds," Emma said.

"Yes. I trust Gerald—and I have not done well when I trusted others. He does have the golden touch, and he is not called Midas Mixton for nothing."

"Will Mr. Mixton be visiting us at Cranley Hall?" Emma inquired politely.

"No. He seldom leaves London. But you will meet him when we go—I should like you to meet him. And you will also meet my mother, who is looking forward to our visit. She took particular care to mention that my brother and his wife hold you in high esteem, Miss Snow." Lord William took a very deep breath. "In fact, I should like to introduce you as my fiancée, if you do not mind."

She gawped at him but said nothing.

"Oh, I know that I have not told your father of my intentions and that this is really quite improper but—"

The door opened. Winkworth, who had undoubtedly been listening at the keyhole, poked his head in. "Would you like a cup of tea, sir?"

"Damnation! No! Not when I am trying to—oh, go away!"

Mrs. Diggory stood on tiptoes to peep over the butler's shoulder.

"Is there anyone else listening at the library door?" Lord William groaned. "I ought to be able to propose in my own house to my own true love, I think—"

"He's proposing!" Mrs. Diggory squeaked to an unseen someone.

"Verra good," came Jamie's reply.

"Carry on, sir." Winkworth grinned and shut

the door. The sound of his measured footsteps was loud indeed, even through the door. "Come along, all of you. We . . . are . . . leaving . . . now. . . ." His voice died away.

Lord William looked helplessly at Emma. "I have made a hash of it, I am afraid."

"No, you have not," she said quietly.

"Then—then—will you consider my proposal? I shall observe all the formalities in due time, inquire of your papa, persuade your mama—whatever it takes."

He gave her a beseeching look, wanting only to sweep her into his arms, but she did not quite meet his gaze. Was that a tear upon her cheek? Hang it, he *was* making a hash of it.

"Emma—dearest Emma—since the day you came to Cranley Hall, it seemed that you had always lived here. I cannot imagine this house without you. I cannot imagine my *life* without you. Marry me, Emma!"

She rose and twined her arms about his neck, kissing him full on the lips. He kissed back, a little breathlessly. "Mmf! Is that—is that a yes?"

"Yes, you fool!"

CHAPTER 18

The very next summer . . .

Emma walked through the rows of rosebushes in the garden, pausing to enjoy the fragrance of a fully blown one before she sat down. She was followed by two cats, one striped and one sand-colored. Wink and Cleo walked just as slowly as she did in the summer heat.

They disappeared under a shrub to find a cool spot. Emma wished she could do the same. She had brought a book and her knitting, as she planned to sit for a while in the arbor that Jamie had constructed of woven branches and twigs. Its arched top kept off the summer sun without being gloomy.

She heard the old gardener swearing in Gaelic somewhere around the side of the house and wondered what he was up to. She set her things on the arbor bench and walked on.

His voice seemed to be coming from the ballroom. Everything at Cranley Hall had been repaired and restored but that. She looked around for Jamie—there he was, yanking long tendrils of ivy from the ballroom walls, one by one.

She saw what she had never been able to see before. The ballroom's walls were built of the same golden Cotswold stone as the house. The ivy rootlets stuck to it with fierce determination.

But Jamie was fiercer. He yanked and pulled and cursed.

Emma came closer. "Mr. Crichton! It looks quite different. I must say, you are working hard."

"Aye."

"Have you seen Lord William?"

"Yer husband is inside the ballroom. The ivy crept through the windows. It is a bluidy awful job to pull it down."

"I will tell Mrs. Crichton to make you some lemonade if you like."

"Aye. She makes verra good lemonade."

Emma smiled. "I know. I will bring a big jug out here so we all can enjoy some."

"But you should not be carrying heavy things." He cast a glance below her sash. "Ask Robbie. Where does he hide? Mary can never find the lad when she needs him."

"Asleep in the hayloft, most likely."

"Then you must ask Susie to help."

"She is cleaning the upstairs windows with Winkworth."

Jamie grinned. "I forgot. They have a funny way of doin' it—her on the inside, scrubbin' away and making faces at him on th' outside. He might fall off th' ladder, the way he laughs."

"They are happy together."

"Cranley Hall is a happy place, my lady."

Emma could add nothing to that statement. She smiled at Jamie and turned her steps to the kitchen where Mrs. Crichton could be seen through the window. The housekeeper waved at her. Emma walked slowly but she got there.

She stepped over the worn stone step and held the railing to go down into the kitchen. When there was no fire in the stove, it was one of the coolest places in the house.

"Could you make lemonade, Mary? Jamie is working hard and the sun is hot."

"Certainly. But please sit down." The housekeeper pulled out a chair and Emma sat down heavily.

"Oh, my." Emma let out her breath with a whoosh. "Perhaps I should not complain. You had five sons."

"They all came in winter, my lady. I cannot imagine what it is like to be great with child in such heat."

"It is most uncomfortable. I can scarcely walk."

Mrs. Crichton nodded understandingly. "It is like that toward the end. But we will take good care of you, never fear. A new babe born at Cranley Hall! It has been many years since we have been so blessed. First you and now—oh!" She stopped herself. "I was not supposed to tell you. Not yet."

"Susie?"

Mrs. Crichton beamed. "Wink is so happy. It was he who told me—and asked me to keep quiet, too."

"I will say nothing of it until they announce it themselves, Mrs. Crichton."

"Thank you, my lady."

She brought a bowl of lemons to the table, cut

each in half and began to squeeze them into a bowl. The sharp fragrance tickled Emma's nose and she sneezed.

"No, no. You shouldn't be sneezing."

"One little sneeze won't make anything happen, Mary."

"Still and all . . ." The housekeeper moved the bowl to the kitchen counter. "You could keep Lord William company. I will bring the lemonade out."

"Oh, very well." Emma rose clumsily with one hand on her back and one resting on the heavy table. She waved away Mary's offer of assistance and made her way out into the sunlight.

Lord William ran to her.

"It is not fair that you can run and I must waddle," she said with a rueful smile.

"Come and look at the ballroom. The ceiling is quite wonderful. One day we will dance under it."

She could not imagine herself moving that quickly ever again. "Very well."

He took her arm to walk with her over the lawn, which Jamie had clipped and rolled to velvet smoothness. He led her inside a tall, glass-paned door that she had thought was a window.

Emma looked up. The crumbling plaster ceiling had been painted a cerulean blue long ago. She could just see the painted stars.

"Oh, my!"

Lord William stood beside her and kicked away lumps of plaster. "There is a great deal of work to be done. But perhaps we will have a ball here next year."

"I hope so." The thought made her sigh with anticipation.

Lord William looked instantly concerned. "Are

you feeling quite well, dearest? Would you like to sit down? There is a chair somewhere about."

"I am all right. Sitting down is not always best. It is too much trouble to get up again."

Lord William nuzzled her neck. "Then shall we dance, my sweet wife? Do you love me as much as I love you?"

"Yes. And yes."

He took her in his arms and they danced . . . very slowly.

More Regency Romance
From Zebra

Embrace the Romance of
Shannon Drake

Discover the Romances of
Hannah Howell

__My Valiant Knight	0-8217-5186-7	$5.50US/$7.00CAN
__Only for You	0-8217-5943-4	$5.99US/$7.50CAN
__Unconquered	0-8217-5417-3	$5.99US/$7.50CAN
__A Taste of Fire	0-8217-7133-7	$5.99US/$7.50CAN
__A Stockingful of Joy	0-8217-6754-2	$5.99US/$7.50CAN
__Highland Destiny	0-8217-5921-3	$5.99US/$7.50CAN
__Highland Honor	0-8217-6095-5	$5.99US/$7.50CAN
__Highland Promise	0-8217-6254-0	$5.99US/$7.50CAN
__Highland Vow	0-8217-6614-7	$5.99US/$7.50CAN
__Highland Knight	0-8217-6817-4	$5.99US/$7.50CAN
__Highland Hearts	0-8217-6925-1	$5.99US/$7.50CAN
__Highland Bride	0-8217-7397-6	$6.50US/$8.99CAN
__Highland Angel	0-8217-7426-3	$6.50US/$8.99CAN

Available Wherever Books Are Sold!

Visit our website at **www.kensingtonbooks.com**.